"No!" b[...]are, and her che[...] [...]ust do what's right."

I stand from the breakfast table. "And according to you, what is that? Die before I'm ready? Grow old in this big house alone?"

"I don't have the answers, but I know you can't lie and hijack someone else's life, their happiness, for your own. *You* get to live the life that's given to *you*." She sighs. "That's it. You take the punches with the wins."

She stares at my lips, and I find myself staring at hers.

"And what sort of wins are you looking for?" I ask.

She says nothing. I'm suddenly thinking about grabbing her and "winning" with her on the table. I'm thinking about putting my mouth on her neck and kissing my way south. I love pushing boundaries, and with her, everything is a boundary.

Before I can process what's happening, I'm stepping around the table, about to go for it.

Wait. What am I doing? She is a virgin, and I am not about to change that. Not that there's anything wrong with taking what I want, as a vampire should, but it simply wouldn't feel right.

OTHER WORKS BY MIMI JEAN PAMFILOFF

COMING SOON!
Baby, Please (OHellNo, #7) ← Yummy football
player with a baby, anyone?
God of Temptation (The Immortal Matchmakers,
Finale) ← For real this time!
Lord King (King Series #7) ← Will King find Mia?
Ultra Mega Love ← What could this be?

THE ACCIDENTALLY YOURS SERIES
(Paranormal Romance/Humor)
Accidentally in Love with…a God? (Book 1)
Accidentally Married to…a Vampire? (Book 2)
Sun God Seeks…Surrogate? (Book 3)
Accidentally…Evil? (Novella, Book 3.5)
Vampires Need Not…Apply? (Book 4)
Accidentally…Cimil? (Novella, Book 4.5)
Accidentally…Over? (FINALE, Book 5)

THE BOYFRIEND COLLECTOR DUET
(New Adult/Suspense)
The Boyfriend Collector, Part 1
The Boyfriend Collector, Part 2

FANGED LOVE
(Standalone/Paranormal/Humor)

THE FATE BOOK DUET
(New Adult/Humor)
Fate Book
Fate Book Two

THE FUGLY DUET
(Contemporary Romance)
fugly
it's a fugly life

THE HAPPY PANTS SERIES
(Standalones/Romantic Comedy)
The Happy Pants Café (Prequel)
Tailored for Trouble (Book 1)
Leather Pants (Book 2)
Skinny Pants (Book 3)

IMMORTAL MATCHMAKERS, INC., SERIES
(Standalones/Paranormal/Humor)
The Immortal Matchmakers (Book 1)
Tommaso (Book 2)
God of Wine (Book 3)
The Goddess of Forgetfulness (Book 4)
Colel (Book 5)
Brutus (Book 6)
God of Temptation (Finale) ← 2021!

THE KING SERIES
(Dark Fantasy/Suspense)
King's (Book 1)
King for a Day (Book 2)
King of Me (Book 3)
Mack (Book 4)
Ten Club (Book 5)
The Dead King (Book 6)
Lord King (Book 7) ← Coming Soon!
Never King's (Book 8) ← Coming 2022

SUITE #45 SERIES by M.O. MACK
(Thriller/Suspense/Action)
She's Got the Guns (Book 1)
She's Got the Money (Book 2)

WISH, a Standalone Novel
(Romantic Comedy)

VAMPIRE MAN

THE LIBRARIAN'S VAMPIRE ASSISTANT SERIES
BOOK 6

MIMI JEAN PAMFILOFF

A Mimi Boutique Novel

www.mimijean.net

Cover Design: Earthly Charms
Developmental Editing: Stephanie Elliot
Copyediting and Proof Reading: Pauline Nolet
Formatting: Paul Salvette

VAMPIRE MAN

CHAPTER ONE

"Nope. Nuh-uh. No way. I'm not going to tell Mr. Nice. *You* tell him," says Dr. Kleen from his office, unaware that the door is ajar. I can hear the damned fool all the way in the waiting room even with my human ears.

Yes, that is correct. *Human* ears. I am an ancient deadly vampire, now trapped in a human shell. *Bleh!* I loathe being so weak and slow moving with all these squishy warm parts.

But perhaps I have gotten ahead of myself due to my rather unpleasant, rapidly evolving medical situation. Allow me to make proper introductions.

My name is Nicephorus, better known in the vampire world as Mr. Nice. My cruelty, strength, and outrageous behavior are the things of legends. The mere mention of my name sends the deadliest creatures running for the hills. *At least, it used to.*

The conversation inside the royal vampire physician's office continues, and I hold my breath to listen.

"You, sir, are the head of the rehumanization project. You will deliver the news, or I will call the king and have you punished." And that would be

Michael Vanderhorst speaking to Dr. Kleen. Vanderhorst is my vampire caretaker. We have a very long history, he and I, none of it pleasant. I plan to murder him soon.

As for this "rehumanization" project, I am certain you are wondering what this is. A fair question. I will get to the answer in a moment, after I ascertain what is happening.

It cannot be good news. I have spent three weeks here in Cincinnati at vampire headquarters, being poked and prodded in the basement lab. They assured me they would find a solution for my predicament, but it appears they have failed. I should have known not to trust the bastards. *Especially Vanderhorst.*

I mentally double down on my plan to pluck out his innards for what he has done, a plan I will keep concealed until the right moment. At present, I need him, and he must believe I am a different person. A changed man.

Of course, a leopard cannot change its spots. Even if I could, I would not wish to. I like being evil. I revel in the destruction of my foes because I understand one very important fact: The world is made up of two types of creatures, and only two. Those who hunt, and those who are eaten.

I do not know about you, my friends, but I prefer a full belly.

I stand and walk to the office door, leaning my ear toward the crack so I do not miss a single word of the conversation.

"Nice and I have a *unique* relationship," Vanderhorst says. "He doesn't seem to trust me, which is why he needs to hear the news from a neutral party."

"You want me," says Kleen, "to tell the meanest vampire ever to walk the earth that we can't help him?"

Can't help me? My gut feels heavy and tight all of a sudden. I place a hand atop my black T-shirt, over the ache, and continue eavesdropping.

Vanderhorst groans. "He can't hurt you. You've seen the bloodwork for yourself. He's no longer a vampire. And we all know he can't remember who he was. No one who's been given the cure can! To them, their vampire lives never happened. Hell, Nice thinks he's a five-year-old kid!"

What fools they are to believe that their little vampirism cure would erase my memories. Unlike the other patients, I remember everything! No silly cure could wipe away who I was born to be. Rotten. Bloodthirsty. Powerful. *Mr. Nice!*

And for the record, I do *not* have the mind of a small child. I simply allow them to believe that because I do not want to reveal I am unchanged on the inside—all part of my master plan. *World domination!*

It is also worth noting I have the body of a spec-tacularly fit twenty-five-year-old male of the modern age. The vitamin supplements, protein shakes, and copious amounts of nutritious meals—lean meats, salads, fresh fruits—have proven successful. My new and improved physique is also part of my master plan.

What was *not* part of it is that I have only been human for five years. Yes, infant body to grown-man body in five years.

Confusing?

You would be correct about that. It is the very reason I am here at vampire headquarters being treated like a lab rat. It is the mystery Vanderhorst is discussing with the royal physician. Why am I aging so fast?

Obviously, we do not know, but we do understand what triggered it: Five years ago, Michael Vanderhorst discovered the cure for vampirism, and I, an ancient vampire, took the first dose.

All right. I *stole* the first dose.

All right, all right. Technically I stole the first fifty doses. I had my reasons. Unfortunately, I was unaware that the vial I drank was meant to be given one drop at a time to one vampire at a time.

I consumed the entire thing.

And that was where the next chapter of my three-hundred-year-long life began. The cure not only removed all traces of vampire blood from my body, but it reverted my human cells back to the equivalent of a two-month-old baby. *Baby Nice* they called me. Me! A deadly villain.

But the suffering did not end there. Oh no, my

friends.

Due to my exorbitantly cruel reputation, no vampire would take me in.

So there I was, unwanted with a fat little baby body, unable to feed or change myself. As the idiot gods of fate would have it, the only vampire willing to house me was Vanderhorst, the man I blame for all this. The man who stole the love of my life, Miriam. The man who keeps getting in the way of my master plan. *World domination!*

And until today, I merely considered my body situation a detour. I'd planned to live as a human until adulthood and then find a vampire to turn me. The do-over I always wanted with a new sexy body! *Mr. Nice two point oh-yes-please.*

Well, except…clearly my plans have encountered a roadblock.

The doctor continues, "Sir, I honestly think we should wait to tell him. I have ten different scientists out in the field, collecting data on everyone who's taken the cure. We're only just beginning to understand the long-term effects and—"

"And what?" Vanderhorst snaps. "You wish to give him false hope? There is no time for that! He must hear the truth—the facts as we know them today. And he needs to hear it from you."

"I don't know…" says the doctor with a groan.

"Fine. Then I'll go do—Nice, how long have you been standing here?" Vanderhorst appears in the doctor's doorway, staring up at me. I am taller than him by several inches at a godlike six feet three.

"Oh, not long, Dad." *God, how I hate calling him that.* Miriam insisted on us being a family, but simply because a man changes your diapers, applies bandages to your boo-boos, midnight feeds you, and cares for you as his own does *not* make him your father!

"Why don't you come inside, son, and have a seat." Vanderhorst gestures for me to enter Dr. Kleen's office. I do not like the way he is looking at me. Dark pity-filled eyes.

I enter, and a sense of gnawing dread pushes through my entrails. It's a windowless room filled with bookshelves, diplomas, and a desk cluttered with *Star Wars* figures. Dr. Kleen was turned around the age of thirteen or fourteen. He never let go of his youth, even though he's about a century old.

I sit and wait for one of the two men to speak, my glorious head of dark long waves toggling back and forth.

Vanderhorst clears his throat and scratches his unshaven jaw. "Son, do you remember our conversation before we came here, about why your body is so much bigger than the other children your age?"

I put on my stupid hat, part of my façade. "You mean, why I had to stop going to the playground?" That place was vile. There had been no hope of gaining a six-pack on such equipment.

"Yes, son." Vanderhorst smiles with affection. Affection I will shove up his ass one day. "That's right. And now the doctors have run all the tests to tell us what is wrong."

"What's wrong with me, Dad?" I say, feigning childlike fear.

"You don't remember this, but you were like me once. A vampire. And vampires are created by an organism that changes our bodies. And five years ago, you took a special medicine—just like I told you before. You don't remember any of it because the medicine makes you forget. Are you following?"

Get on with it, you putz! Before I tear off your lips. "Yes, Dad."

"Good, because what I'm going to say will be difficult to…to…"

Dear vampire gods. Are his eyes actually filling with tears? How could my Miriam marry this wimp over me? I will have to show her what a real man looks like and steal her back!

Vanderhorst sucks in a deep breath and continues, "We can't stop your aging. I am very, very sorry." He hangs his head and stares at the floor.

If I were a fool, I would believe his act; however, I have been around for far too long. Vanderhorst couldn't be happier to get rid of me.

"I-I don't know what I'm going to tell your mother." Vanderhorst turns into a blubbering fool. "Miriam loves you so much."

Blood mingles with his tears, and suddenly my heart is beating faster. I have never seen a vampire cry bloody tears. It is said that it only happens when a vampire loses a piece of their soul forever.

I start looking for the red food coloring. Surely, he must have a bottle hidden in his hand.

"I am so sorry, sir." Dr. Kleen pats his shoulder. "I promise we won't give up looking for answers."

Vanderhorst's chest jerks with a hiccup. "Thank you, Dr. Kleen."

I cannot believe these two and their theatrics. They are very good at pretending to care for me. But aren't all vampires excellent actors?

"Dad, I have a question," I say.

"Yes, son?" He drags his fist across his cheek, mopping up the tears.

"Can't *you* turn me into a vampire again? It would stop my aging, right?"

Vanderhorst looks at me with wide dark eyes, and the doctor follows suit.

Suddenly, the gravity of the situation hits. Something is wrong. Something else I have not planned for.

Standing over me, Vanderhorst places his hands on my shoulders. "I am sorry, but I cannot turn you. By order of the king, any vampire who gives you their blood will be put to death. He thinks you are destined to be evil again." Vanderhorst looks away, the red tears reaching his crisp white collar.

For the first time in my long existence, I feel confused. "You're-you're saying I will never be a vampire again?"

Vanderhorst looks down at the floor again, unable to face me. "No. And with the speed of your aging, you will be dead within a year."

CHAPTER TWO

I have less than twelve months to live? And according to their calculations, I have but a few weeks remaining before my sublime, masculine body begins to deteriorate into a wrinkled piece of man-jerky.

Lying back in the lounge chair by the pool of our spacious, resort-like mansion in Phoenix, I take a swig of whiskey straight from the bottle and stare up at the starry Arizona night sky. Miriam is inside the house, inconsolable. She and my ten-year-old "sister" Stella have been crying since I returned from Cincinnati with Vanderhorst.

I can understand why Miriam is upset. Deep in her heart, she knows we were meant to be together. As for Vanderhorst, perhaps he will miss having such a fearsome foe.

"Well, congratulations, Vanderhorst!" I raise the bottle to the sky. "You won. She is your fanged love."

"Fanged…love?" Vanderhorst's voice comes from behind me. "But we banned that book from our home. Your mother prohibited you from even hearing the title. How do you know about it?"

Fanged Love is a vampire romance series Miriam

loves. I pretended to be obsessed with it, too, when I was a vampire. No offense to the authors, two vampire-obsessed women, Mimi Jean Pamfiloff and Kylie Gilmore, but it is a little ridiculous to believe such a treacherous being such as myself would truly be a fan of a mushy love story. *Blech!* Nonetheless, I had been compelled to tell many lies in order to create the legendary persona of Mr. Nice.

You see, friends, despite all his faults and darkness, my maker, Narcissismo, taught me one valuable lesson: Vampires fear what they do not understand. So always keep them guessing.

Vampires are also savages, and if you want to survive in their world, if you want true power, they must tremble in your presence. That requires tall tales of glorious brutality to be circulated for centuries, repeated so many times they become fact.

For example, most believe I am over a thousand years old and a general from the Byzantine army. *Puffery!* I am actually of Spanish and Greek descent, only three hundred years old, give or take a few decades. Most also believe I am insane, eccentric, and unpredictable. Also untrue. I am simply evil, conniving, and merciless.

In any case, the Mr. Nice façade I've worked so hard to create is now useless. There is no point in pretending any longer. No more strange accents. No more flamboyant lace and leather outfits. No more terrorizing the vampire world with my obscure threats or unconventional requests. *Milk a cat and make me some cheese!*

I take another swig from the bottle, ignoring his question. "Miriam was always meant to be with me, and nothing will change that. Her heart knows you can't protect her like I can."

Like the time she was about to be slaughtered by Michael's maker, Cluentius Boethius, the evilest vampire ever to live besides me. He was my hero. But I love Miriam, and when I saw she was about to die because Vanderhorst had failed to protect her, it drove me to action. I killed Cluentius and swept her away to safety, vowing to never let her fall into Vanderhorst's inept, feeble hands again. Vanderhorst eventually found us and got her back. *Grrr...*

Vanderhorst steps into the glowing aqua light of the swimming pool, his jaw hanging open. "I knew it. I knew you remembered everything!" He spins in place, shaking his head. "I can't believe it! All this time you were *him*! You are still Mr. Nice!"

I stand from the lounge chair and stare him down, feeling the whiskey run freely through my veins. "That is correct, *Daaad*. I remember everything before I took your ridiculous cure. I remember how you nearly shat yourself when I used to enter a room. I remember it all, and trust me when I say I will never forget the long nights I have spent in Miriam's arms these past years."

He winces. "Miriam was being your mother. Have you no decency?"

I flash a sadistic smile. "You, the Executioner, known for his savagery during the Great War, dare to judge me?" He slaughtered thousands of evil vampires, many of them my close friends.

"What I did was necessary for a better world, for humans and vampires alike. What you've done is vile. It's despicable!"

"Michael? I heard yelling. What's going on?" Miriam emerges from the house in her pink sweater and jeans. Her big brown eyes are puffy and red. Her blonde hair is in a messy ponytail.

"He is a fake." Vanderhorst points at me. "As I told you a thousand times, woman. He is still Mr. Nice, the very vampire who stole you from me when you were pregnant with our child."

For the record, Stella is a half vampire and was born shortly after I saved Miriam from death. But Stella received around-the-clock nannying and security. It was the sort of childhood I wish I'd had. No one protected me when Narcissimo murdered my parents. No one made sure I was fed and safe. I lived like a ship rat, surviving off scraps while tethered to a vicious vampire.

Ah, but my sweet Miriam and her child were treated like queens. I even changed Miriam into a vampire so she could be strong and always protect herself and Stella no matter what. She was a little miffed about that, but I knew with time she would come to appreciate my gift and see that I did it out of love.

Of course, Vanderhorst just had to come along and ruin everything with his ridiculous "rehumanization" project. *Always have to be the hero, don't you, Vanderhorst?* Miriam took the cure—one drop only—the same day as I and ended up back with him. *Blech!*

Luckily for her, though, I am no quitter. After they brought me into their home, I found myself in a unique situation to bond with Miriam in a new way: snuggled close to her bosom while being bottle-fed, bathed with her warm loving hands, and taken for long walks in the stroller. *Good times.* Even better, my constant care took attention away from Vanderhorst. Ha!

Miriam's eyes float to mine, searching for the truth, but I have danced this tango of lies many times. "No, Mom. He's lying. Dad's just jealous of this man he calls Mr. Nice, but I don't remember him. I don't know who he is."

As I'm preparing to pound the final nail in Vanderhorst's coffin, a beep sounds on my phone. Miriam's jeans pocket lights up.

I look down at my cell on the small table beside the lounge chair. The text is from Vanderhorst.

Huh? I pick it up and read it. The message says, *Gotcha!* And there's a sound bite attached. *No. No. No!* He recorded our conversation just now and sent it to Miriam.

I glare at him, taking note of the joyful gleam in his eyes. My heart blisters with rage. "How could you?"

"No." Vanderhorst steps forward, pressing his chest to mine. "How could *you*?"

"I'll kill you. I'll shred you to pieces and—"

"Bring it, human," he snarls. "Just give me one excuse to remove your head."

"Michael, no. Don't hurt him. It's not even a fair fight." Miriam grabs his arm. "Let's just…get some sleep and discuss this in the morning like civilized people."

Vanderhorst backs off, his face red, nostrils flaring. He is upset because Miriam protected me.

"There. You see? She understands the true complexity of our love," I say.

Miriam slowly turns, hate filling her eyes. "Yes. What I felt for you *was* love. Love for a tiny, helpless baby who needed a family. And I don't know what you feel for me, but I guarantee it isn't love."

The rage in her soft brown eyes sends a cold shiver down my spine. I watch as she and Vanderhorst enter the house and slam the back door. The gesture feels big, as if they are shutting the door on me forever.

Is it possible I have miscalculated? Does Miriam truly not care for me?

No, impossible. The Nice does not make mistakes.

Then why do I suddenly feel so alone?

CHAPTER THREE

After a long and restless night on the lounge chair outside, my sore human body and I have awoken with a new perspective on things.

All is not lost! World domination is still within my grasp if I play my cards right.

Regarding the ban on me becoming a vampire again, I can appeal to the king's senses. In other words, I will blackmail him.

Little-known fact: "Dad" is the true vampire king, the original Michael Vanderhorst. But five years ago, around the time I took the cure, Michael wished to vacate the throne without destabilizing the vampire kingdom, which had just gone through a dicey coup. He convinced his twin, the reclusive Freddy Vanderhorst, to take his place so that Michael could live a quiet peaceful life with Miriam, Stella, and me.

Now Freddy sits on the throne, pretending to be Michael, and the entire vampire world believes that Miriam left the king for his kinder twin brother. *The old twin switcharoo!* Such a cliché if you ask me, but also my win.

I will threaten to disclose their little twin secret

if they do not turn me, which solves that problem.

As for Miriam, I have decided the best course of action is to tell her my side of things. No doubt, Vanderhorst has filled her head with lies. When she hears the truth, she will forgive me and see that he is nothing but a weak man, unworthy of her love.

I jostle the back door and find it unlocked. Miriam must've left it open for me so I wouldn't miss breakfast. She loves cooking for me. Farm-fresh eggs, organic orange juice, whole wheat toast, strawberry protein smoothie, sausage, and my vitamins. She knows I must eat well to fuel my powerful, manly body.

I walk into the kitchen, noting the dimmed lights. The air lacks the scent of a homecooked meal and coffee. The house is quiet.

"Miriam? Vanderhorst? Stella?"

No one answers. Something is off.

Panicked, I rush to the library, which is situated in a separate wing of the house. Three stories high with a stained-glass dome for a ceiling, it is filled to the brim with thousands of books. This is where Miriam spends most of her time.

No one? The room is empty. But where could they be?

Of course! The other library! Miriam's parents founded a public library downtown. Vanderhorst has been running things while she's been occupied with me and Stella, but perhaps today is one of her book fairs.

I will go to her and make my case, but first I must bathe and look presentable. I rush upstairs to my room and stop on the red carpet. My entire room is decorated for a prince. *Dark prince.*

There is a note on my bed, and I recognize the handwriting as Vanderhorst's.

Dear Mr. Nice,

You are a monster who has lived up to every despicable word that has been said about you over the centuries.

We offered you a home and a family. You betrayed us all—the only ones willing to give you a second chance.

Words cannot express our disappointment. Maybe soon, when you take your last breath, you will comprehend what you have done and what you have given up.

We will not return until after you are dead and gone. Please water my plants.

Goodbye,
Michael

P.S. Miriam never wishes to speak to you again. She has texted you a video in case you have delusions about it. Stella hopes you die on an iceberg of loneliness.

I drop the note on the bed. *This cannot be.* Miriam never wants to speak to me again? Nor Stella? I have been her playmate for longer than I care to admit. *Does anyone know how hard it is to dress a Barbie?*

Traitor!

I pull my phone from my pocket and check my messages. I see something from Miriam.

I must've missed it while passed out. I had way too much whiskey last night for a five-year-old. No, no. I am not actually five. Think of me as a very old soul trapped in a fresh new body that can't hold its liquor.

I tap the message and stop it before it plays in its entirety. One look at Miriam's red face tells me all I need to know. Vanderhorst has told the truth in his letter. He has won. And my family has abandoned me.

ॐ ॐ

I spend the next several hours in shock, mostly because I do not know how to cook, so I am relegated to eating Cocoa Puffs.

Do they really expect me to care for myself?

Soon I will be old and gray and unable to walk. Who will wash my clothes? Do the grocery shopping? Pay the bills? I have plenty of money stashed away, so that is not a concern, but I do not understand how they think I can perform all these menial tasks on my own.

I'm a vampire! Vampires don't do chores. They have human slaves or they make weaker vampires do the work in exchange for protection. It has been so for centuries.

I groan, trying to wrap my head of thick, long, wavy locks around this conundrum. *Hmmm...* I could still go to the king and threaten to expose his secret, but he has probably been warned already. He might throw me in vampire jail to live out my final months.

I think and think hard.

Surely there must be a vampire out there willing to turn me, if not for money, then to spite the king. Not all five hundred eighty-two societies support him.

"Society" is our term for coven, mostly because vampires hide in plain sight, living among humans, operating businesses or working for companies.

And in order to have a place to conduct vampire business, each coven officially registers with the human regulatory bodies as some sort of nonprofit, generally one that has the name "society" in it.

For example, here in Phoenix, we are the Arizona Society of Sunshine Love. Officially, it is a private organization dedicated to driving awareness of the benefits of sunshine. Unofficially, it was some vampire's idea of a joke. Vampires do not enjoy or benefit from the sun, though we can and do tolerate it all the time. It merely weakens us.

Another well-known coven is the Cincinnati Historical Society of Original Family Members—a historical preservation club. Also a little vampire humor, since vampires are preserved history.

My most recent coven was founded by yours truly, the New Orleans Spicy Gumbo Society. I am quite proud of the name since we refer to humans from that region as spicy gumbo. They are quite flavorful.

I stare into my empty cereal bowl while seated at the kitchen counter. All these thoughts of vampire culture make me bodysick. It's like being homesick, but for my old vampire body. I used to love drinking blood. Especially the sensation right before the meal is ending when the human's arms are desperately flailing about.

I sigh with longing. *I must find a way to become a vampire again.*

I get up and go into the study, finding a pen and paper. I make a list of every ally, every enemy of the Vanderhorsts, and every evil vampire. Surely someone on this list will turn me before my young, healthy body breaks down to middle age. *Bleh!* I must be young forever or nothing at all.

I go up to my room, pack my bag, and say goodbye to this family, this house, and this burning hellhole called Arizona.

I do not need any of it. I do not need Miriam, Vanderhorst, or Stella. I will find my own way through this mess and rise once again to my place at the top of vampire society.

With a suitcase in hand, I stop in the foyer, realizing I cannot fly.

No, I mean I cannot fly commercial. I do not possess the proper documentation. I cannot fly the other way either. Vampires can only run fast. I cannot even do that at present.

I go to the five-car garage and smile. *Sorry, Vanderhorst. But you left it behind.* I grab the keys from the hook on the wall and climb into the brand-new silver Mercedes G-Class with tinted windows. He loves this boxy SUV beast more than he loves his first-edition books.

Mine now, Vanderhorst. A tiny consolation prize for all that he has taken from me.

CHAPTER FOUR

After a six-hour drive, I enter the Rusty Nail, a seedy bar in El Paso, Texas. I have not been here in decades, but my old friend Bob the Impaler runs it, and he owes me a few favors. Out of everyone on the list, he is by far my oldest and closest friend.

There was this one time we traveled on a cruise liner during the 1920s. We had such a time! Drinking and throwing bodies overboard. Every day, ten more passengers would be reported missing. It was utter pandemonium. Eventually, the passengers threw the captain overboard because he was unable to give them answers or protect them. I always did enjoy watching others take the blame for my actions.

Dressed in my leather pants and black velvet jacket, I enter the dark, smokey bar located in a run-down strip mall next to a grimy bowling alley. The Rusty Nail is a certifiable dump—dirty concrete floor, chipped-up tables, ratty vinyl-covered chairs. A few drunk customers sit slumped over at the bar, and a country tune plays on the jukebox.

The door closes behind me, and I inhale deeply, savoring the sinister atmosphere. "It is just as a remember." I even catch the faint scent of copper in the air. Someone has died here recently. Likely one of those cartel types.

So delicious. It is a well-known fact that the more evil a person is, the spicier their blood. Vampires love anything hot, including chili peppers, raw or in a sauce. Yes, we—I mean vampires—eat human food. These days, I am stuck with bland but healthy meals. My five-year-old tongue is not accustomed to complex flavors or the fiery heat of the coveted ghost pepper.

I cannot wait to return to my old diet. Also, I must constantly work out to maintain my six-pack. It is exhausting looking so masculine. The sooner I am immortal, the better!

"Nice, is that you?"

I look over at Bob, who has just come from the back room. He has golden brown skin, straight black hair down to his waist, and wears a cowboy hat. I am not sure of his actual age, but he has the face of a twenty-year-old. The ladies love his rugged demeanor and long silky hair. I was always jealous of his strong physique. When I was turned the first time, I had been malnourished by my vampire captor. *Jealous no more.*

"Bob! *Jesss…* It is I, your old friend Nicephorus," I say in my crazy Mr. Nice accent, which no one could ever pin down. *Always keep 'em guessing*, as Narcissismo used to say.

We embrace, but Bob squeezes me too hard. I

suck up the pain, not wanting him to see my weakness.

He releases me, and I note an odd look in his dark eyes.

"It has been many years," he says, the look growing more nefarious, complete with eye twitches. "You smell so delicious." He squeezes my bicep. "And my, my, my, how you've filled out. So juicy." He licks his lips. "And your scent…" He throws back his head and inhales. "Spicy!"

My eyes go wide, and I step back, holding out my hands. "Bob, no. I am *chor* old friend, Mr. Nice. Do *choo* not recall the cruise liner? The redheaded twins we shared *zat* first night? How about the time we went horse shopping to stock your ranch? I picked out *zi* white stallion and gave it to you as a gift. You named him Moonshine."

From the hungry look in his eyes, I can tell that Bob the Impaler is not hearing a word I've said. The stomach brain is in control now.

I dare not run, because it will only make him want to chase me. "Fine, I'm leaving, Bob. But know this, I will soon be a vampire again—a hundred times more powerful than before. I will remember this moment when you turned your back on your best friend."

"Go!" he growls. "And do not return here again, or I will eat you. Toes first."

Jeez… That's a little dark. I turn and leave, my face and palms sweating profusely. I cannot believe it, but I felt genuinely worried just now. It is an emotion I haven't experienced in centuries. My heart is thumping, like a hammer in my chest, my head feels light, and I need to piss. Rather badly.

I head down the dark sidewalk, the warm night air offering little comfort as I attempt to process what just happened. It never occurred to me that my dark heart and evil soul would make me irresistible to my own kind. The spiciest, most delectable treat on two legs ever to live.

But I am still a vampire on the inside. One of them! All Bob saw was my blood. To him I was Mr. Nice-and-Fresh Meat.

I wonder if Vanderhorst was ever tempted to nibble on me.

Of course he had been. If I were a vampire, I would want a bite of me. So what kept him from acting if he could smell my spicy blood all along? Probably his ridiculous moral code. Wimp!

I decide to make one more attempt at contacting an old friend, though I do make the strategic choice to skip a few names on my list. The ones I used to admire for their heartless ways are a no-go. It would likely end up a repeat of Bob.

But that still leaves eleven names, and one is in Houston, a ten-hour drive.

The next evening, after being forced to accept my

human need for sleep, I finally arrive to Houston.

Julia is a madam and runs a famous whorehouse in Texas, though it is strictly limited to immortals. Unless you are on the menu.

I park along the curb and unload from the SUV to stretch my tired body. My black leather pants are stuck to my ass, and I make a note to change into jeans if this visit proves unsuccessful. Leather pants and vampire skin are like peanut butter and jelly. Perfect together. But human skin creates moisture. *I think my balls are chafed.*

I tug on my wrinkled black button-down shirt and head to the darkened front porch of the home. For lack of a better term, the place looks like a crack house—weeds in the front yard, broken windows covered with cardboard, garbage bags piled up on the side. It is the type of neighborhood where no one asks questions and people mind their own business.

I ring the doorbell and notice someone looking at me through the peephole. "Julia! It is I, *zi* Mr. Nice. I have *zi* business *propoosal* for you!"

The door flies open, revealing Julia in a long black dress. She has shiny red curls just past her shoulders and bright green eyes. I believe she is about two hundred years old, turned by the famous Madam Frenchie, who died several decades ago in a tragic wood-chipping accident. Frenchie had a tree trimming business on the side—part of her human cover story. All vampires are required to have one.

Human papers, social security number, and an official source of income commensurate to their standard of living. I believe Julia's official occupation is interior decorator. A very, very bad one.

"Mr. Nice, such a lovely surprise." She flashes a set of sharp fangs with bright red lipstick smudges. "Won't you come in."

"I warn you, I smell *varrry* delectable, so do not even think of eating me. Not until you've heard my *propoosal*."

She dips her head, stepping aside so I can enter. "I have just dined on tender spunky woman and am quite full. You are safe."

"Excellent." I enter the living room, and the scent of death hits my nose. Out of respect I maintain a smile, but I want to retch. "I believe your inventory might be a little old?" I glance at a thin woman in a T-shirt and skirt slumped over in the armchair next to the sofa. Her skin is blue. Yesterday's meal.

"Oh, that." Julia swipes a hand through the air. "Garbage day is Thursday. I'll toss her out then."

Nasty. Today is Monday.

She goes on, "I have some fresh ones in the back room. Just arrived today." Julia's green eyes light up with excitement. "Oh. I also have a shipment from the south. Not spicy, but I seem to remember you like Mexican. Care for a nibble? You still eat people, yes?"

This is a prime example of how my Mr. Nice

persona functions. Julia knows I am human but assumes I am still just as wicked and depraved as ever, running around consuming people. Because that is exactly what an evil man would do. It is also the sort of lie I feed to maintain my feared status among vampires.

"No, *sank* you," I say. "I've already eaten. Had a mini-mart clerk on the way over." I pat my stomach. Really, I had a turkey sandwich with extra pickles and lettuce.

"May I interest you in some wine, then?"

"*Jessss*…Thank you." We go to the kitchen, which, now that I am seeing it with human eyes, looks like a diseased war zone. Dried blood on the floor, dirty dishes piled high on the counters, rat droppings on the windowsill.

Julia grabs a dirty glass from the counter, fills it with some red wine in a box from the putrid-smelling refrigerator, and hands me the glass.

First of all, no one refrigerates red wine. Second of all, what self-respecting vampire drinks anything from a box? Third, this glass looks like it hasn't been washed in two hundred years. I doubted I would have cared as a vampire. Cooties and grime do not scare us. Mortality changes your perspective on all that.

I thank her and hold the glass in my hand, away from my face. "As I said, I have a *propoosal* for you."

"How much?"

I stare.

"How much?" she repeats. "We all got the message from the king. I know he's prohibited anyone from turning you. So how much will you pay me to do it?"

Ah, I knew Julia would be the right choice. She speaks the language of money. "Name *chor* price."

"I want a thousand dollars."

I try not to laugh. This is the thing about some vampires, the older ones, anyway. They have no concept of inflation. They still think a soda pop costs a nickel.

"And I want a new house," she says. "This place is falling apart, and it's being condemned."

"Any house in particular?" I ask.

"You have that sweet pad in New Orleans. I want it."

That could be problematic. I rented it out to some Irish vampires. A one-hundred-year lease. I hadn't been living there for a while and felt it was best to have the place occupied. Also, it simply makes financial sense. I personally own over four hundred properties, most managed by a firm. I am quite the investor.

I dip my head in agreement. "I will have to come to an understanding with *zi* current residents, but I'm sure it can be done. The house is yours," I say.

"Great. So, you want to do this now?"

"*Jesss*…That would be wonderful." The process is quite easy. I must drink some of her blood, and then my heart must stop. Death.

Death. Death. My heart starts pumping faster. I do not fear death, but at the same time, the human part of me is a little uncomfortable with the idea of pain. "I need a moment. Bathroom is…?"

"Right through there. To the left." Julia points toward the doorway.

"I'll be right back."

"I'll wait in my bedroom." She winks. "You remember where that is, yes?"

"*Jesss…*" I wink. We had a few fun times in there. Mostly back when she was running her ten-for-one specials. Ten humans and one hell of a fun night!

I turn and head down the hallway to find the bathroom. I've never been in here before. Surprisingly, it is the only room in the house that isn't filthy, with an all-pink tile floor and counters and a blue shower curtain. *Yep. The worst interior decorator ever.*

I relieve myself and wash my hands, staring at my face in the mirror. I am still not used to my reflection. Gone are my hollow cheeks and sunken eyes. My long skinny neck has been replaced by a normal-looking one that slopes down into strong shoulders and a powerful chest. My full lips and dark eyes are the same though. Also, I can grow quite the beard now.

I rub my scruffy jaw and pat some water on the back of my neck, calming myself for what is about to happen. I am excited to be immortal again, to run with the wind through my hair, terrorizing the vampire community as Mr. Nice. *And then...world domination!*

My return will create shock waves through every society. Then I will begin gathering support to take down the Vanderhorst brothers. When news of their twin scheme spreads, vampires will demand justice. I will be there to deliver it.

Suddenly, I note a muffled whimper behind the blue shower curtain. I go over and pull it back, finding a petite female crouched in a ball.

She immediately sees me and sticks out her hands. "Please, please don't hurt me."

"Why would I hurt you?"

"You're one of them."

Not yet. "No," I say.

Her warm brown eyes go wide with hope. "Help me. Please help me get out of here."

"But we must all die, woman. It is part of life." I myself plan to die for a second time in a few moments.

"She has no right to do this to me or anyone here. We have families. We have feelings."

I seriously doubt these "guests" have families. Not anymore. Julia is quite keen on taking everyone from Granny to Tiny Tim when she fills up her inventory. She once nabbed an entire Amish community, horse buggies and all. But that was long ago when she used to cater this fantastic vampire festival in Romania. She'd make sure there was a wide selection of blood to choose from, brought in from all over the world.

The woman lunges for my hand. "Please don't leave me here. Please, I'm begging you. I want to go to school and fall in love. I just want to see my mom and dad and little sister again."

Mom and dad and little sister. The words send a spike of pain through my heart. Suddenly, I'm thinking of Miriam, Stella, and that despicable Vanderhorst. I see them sitting around the dinner table, trying to make me laugh so I'll open my mouth and eat my strained peas. Stella would tickle me until I could not help but open up. I came to enjoy our little games.

I shake my head to dislodge the memory. "Family is overrated."

"Why would you say that?" She looks at me with pity.

"Sorry. I cannot help you." I puff out my wide chest. "You belong to Julia's inventory now, and she decides your fate."

I leave the bathroom and slam right into Julia.

"Who are you speaking to?" she asks.

"One of your meals is hiding in *zi* shower."

Julie goes in and pulls the curtain back all the way. "There you are! Mr. Romanovich ordered you special and will be here any moment. Go get cleaned up and back to your pen."

Romanovich. My entrails twist into a knot. Mr.

Romanovich has been around for a very long time. Russian oligarch turned mobster turned vodka producer. They call him Nails mostly because he enjoys poking holes in his meals with a giant spike. Kind of like making a fountain.

You see, friends, here is the thing about vampires: There is Vanderhorst's vampire world of laws and rules, where vampires are only permitted to eat bad humans on an approved list maintained by their society. That world is neat and clean and orderly. Then there is the other side: The dark hidden world of vampires, where rules mean nothing. They do what they want when they want. And they are good at not getting caught by the vampire authorities. Mostly because bad vampires protect one another, but also because vampires are adept at evading detection.

My point is that some vampires are too low and despicable even for my taste. Nails is one such vampire.

Julia grabs the young woman by her long dark hair and drags her from the bathroom. "Back to your pen!"

The woman cries, and suddenly I have a strange feeling in my chest. For some odd reason, I do not wish her to die. "How much?"

"Sorry?" Julia asks.

"How much for *zi* girl?"

"Sorry, she's not for sale. Romanovich already paid for her, and I do not want to disappoint my best customer."

"But you know what he'll do to her," I argue.

Julia shrugs. "What do you care?" She then smiles. "But don't worry. I have another just like her. Maybe a little sweeter, but same age." Julia drags the girl to a room across the hall and shoves her in, closing the door with a thud. "And don't come out until I call you, or you know what will happen!"

I am unsure of what to do. Seems wrong to leave anyone in Nails's hands.

"Come on now." Julia waves me toward her bedroom. "I've got a lot of work to do if I'm going to get rid of all my inventory and move my business." Julia disappears inside.

I hesitate.

"You coming?" she calls out.

"Yes." I see the dark-haired woman peeking out from the other room. I can hear several people whispering inside.

If I wait until after I'm changed to help her, it'll be too late. The transformation usually takes a few hours.

I look at the woman with the beautiful brown eyes and pouty lips. Then at Julia's doorway. Woman. Doorway. Woman. Doorway. I walk over to Julia's door and shut it. "Run! Hurry! I will hold the door!"

The woman from the shower dashes from the other room, followed by eight or nine more women.

They bolt for the front door, yelling for help.

"Open this door, Nice! Open it right now!" Julia yells.

I know I cannot hold it long. I am strong for a human, but no match for her. The moment I let go, she will kill me.

The door handle turns, and I lose my grip. The door flies open.

I smile down at Julia, whose face is flaming red.

"Oops. I guess your humans got away." I shrug. "So, you still wish to have that money and a house in New Orleans?"

Julia flashes her fangs and growls. "You're a dead man, Nice." She reaches for me so quickly I do not have time to process what is happening. The room goes dark.

CHAPTER FIVE

"Hey, wake up. Wake up. Are you all right?" a soft female voice whispers.

I open my eyes to find the pretty young woman from the shower crouched over me, tapping my cheek, her big eyes filled with worry.

"Where am I?" I grumble, noting wet grass underneath me and trees all around. It is still night—a full moon now—and I feel weak and dizzy.

"We're in a park. A few blocks from that house."

"What happened?" I ask.

"That crazy redhead grabbed you and started drinking from your neck. You must've tasted really good because she was making all these noises. Num, num, num."

I sit up slowly and place my hand over my neck. The skin is wet and raw. I can tell the spot was gnawed on.

"Careful. Easy there." The woman helps me stay upright.

"How do you know what was done to me?" I saw her leave the house screaming.

"The other women and I ran into the street

right when a patrol car was passing. I flagged the officer down and told him there was a murder happening in the house. He went in and shot at that vampire woman because she wouldn't let go of you. Then she fled."

Wow. What luck. "But why are we here?"

"That Romanovich guy showed up, and the cop started shooting at him, too. After that, it was all a blur. I pulled you to your feet, and we ran. You passed out here."

I do not recall any of it. "Thank you for…for saving me."

"You saved me first. My name is Brandi, by the way."

In the distance, I hear sirens. I imagine the home is now surrounded by police.

"Do you think it's safe to go back there?" Brandi asks.

"Why would you want to go back?"

"The police'll want a statement, right? I mean, that woman needs to be caught."

I am too drowsy to laugh. "If you tell the authorities you were taken by a vampire, they will lock you up."

"But the things she did in that house to all those people! She has to be stopped."

By whom? The only ones capable are vampires, and I am not about to rat out Julia to the vampire authorities. I'd be labeled a snitch for all eternity.

"You are safe. Count your blessings." As for myself, I do not understand what got into me. I was so close to having what I wanted. A vampire willing to change me. Immortality once again.

I sigh. Soon word will spread among the seedy vampire masses that I betrayed Julia to save a human meant for slaughter. They will say I lost my spine, that I am weak. Instead of following me, they will laugh when I disclose my plan to overthrow the king. Vampires do not follow weaklings.

Why did I do that? Why! I look at the young woman with long dark hair, a round face, and soulful eyes. She is no different than many I have killed with nary a second thought. What compelled me to save her?

"Are you able to drive?" I grumble.

"Yes."

"Please fetch the silver Mercedes SUV parked one block down from the house. I will need to find a room for the night and lots of Gatorade." I hand her the keys from my pocket and flop back down on the wet grass. The moon is spinning above me.

"Thank you for saving me. I mean it," she says.

"My pleasure," I mutter dryly.

"By the way, you haven't told me your name."

I no longer deserve the name Mr. Nice or Nicephorus—those belong to a cold, heartless, *respectable* vampire.

I was born Steviuus Nicephorus Racker, named after my great-great-great-grandfather—a Byzantine general. I was merely the son of a humble spice merchant, which is why my childhood consisted of traveling in northern Africa from one small village to another while my father purchased spices. He would eventually sell them to the ships bound for the north. That was how we encountered Narcissismo. He was a ship merchant.

"You may call me Racker," I say. Racker was what my maker called me when I was but his pathetic human pet. It is the name I deserve now after tonight.

"Racker, nice to meet you. I'll be right back."

I give Brandi the thumbs-up, unable to do much more than that. I have no idea what will happen to me now.

Sleep. I will sleep. Tomorrow will be a new day.

ॐ ॐ

The next morning, I wake at a roadside motel just outside Houston. I vaguely recall us pulling in last night after I had Brandi procure food and drink.

I look over at the other bed. Brandi is still here, passed out and snoring in a way that no lady ever should. *Like a congested boar.*

The pleasant news is that I have to piss like a racehorse. A good sign because it means I am rehydrated.

I get to my feet and trudge to the bathroom, where I look in the mirror. "What is that!" A gray hair. "No, no, no." I lean forward and pluck it out.

"What's wrong?" Brandi stumbles into the doorway, her brown locks a wild mess.

"Nothing." I do not believe in whining. I am still a vampire, at least on the inside, and vampires do not cry over one silly gray hair. "I was merely shocked by my handsome reflection. Happens a lot."

"Errr...are you feeling okay?" she asks.

"Of course."

"And the neck?"

I turn my head and inspect the puncture marks surrounded by deep purple. "I've had worse." My maker used to find it amusing to drain me to the point of near death and then heal me with his blood, only to repeat the cruel action. At the time, I did not know that had I died with his blood in my veins, I would have turned. I could have killed myself and been free of him long before.

"That sounds pretty awful."

"Yes. But what is life without pain?" I say.

She winces. "It's called a good life."

I shrug.

"So what will you do now? Where's home?" she asks.

"I do not have a home."

"No home? No family?" She sounds surprised.

"No."

"A job?"

"No," I reply.

"And the car?"

"A gift from an acquaintance."

She nods, looking like she doesn't entirely believe me. "Well, I know it's a lot to ask after what you did for me, but would you be willing to drive me home? My family has to be worried sick."

"Where do you live?"

"Missouri. That vampire woman took me from a bus. I was on my way home from University of Texas for summer."

Lucky her. If Brandi had been with her family, they would all be dead by now.

"I am sorry, Brandi, but I cannot take you to your family. I have matters to attend to." Mostly facing my impending doom and old age. "I will buy you an airline ticket."

"I don't have my ID. When that *thing* took me, I didn't have a chance to grab my purse."

"I will pay for a hotel until your family can come get you."

"You want to leave me alone?" Her big brown eyes tear, and her plump little lower lip quivers.

They do not sway me. "A bus ticket, then."

"Bus?" Her worried expression turns into a crumbling mess of sobs. "No buses."

"I understand that is where Julia found you—"

"Please don't say her name." Brandi covers her face and cries inconsolably.

"She won't take you again. I mean, yes, she could, but the chances are quite slim."

"Oh God. Oh God. She'll come for me. She

said she would if I ran. She said she'd find me and kill my little sister and parents."

That is Brandi's problem, not mine, but something stops me from saying so. "Then what do you propose? Because I have urgent business. It cannot wait." Mostly finding a dark hole to crawl into where I may die in peace.

"What could be more important than getting me safely to my family after what I've been through?" She waves a hand through the air. "I mean, I get that you're some perverse vampire lover, but you wouldn't have saved me if you didn't have a heart."

Oddly, I find offense with her words. "I am not a vampire lover. I simply love being a vampire."

"You? You're a vampire?"

"No. I was, though. For a very long time."

"I don't understand."

"I was cured, but that doesn't matter." I wave a dismissive hand through the air.

"Hold on, Racker." She grabs my arm. "You were a vampire, and now you want to be one again, don't you?"

She must've overheard part of my conversation with Julia last night. What she doesn't know is that I blew my chance. Now I am going to die. "My dear woman, the time for your incessant questions has ended. Our time together must also come to an end. I saved you from Julia, but my obligation ends here."

"You owe me, Racker. I didn't have to come back. But I did."

"And?"

Brandi lifts her shirt and shows me her breasts. No, friends, it is not what you think. This is not a request for Mardi Gras beads. The soft fleshy mounds are covered with bite marks, and there is a tattoo of a black bat right across the left breast. It covers the entire nipple and extends several inches in both directions.

I know what it means. She does not have to tell me. Julia intended to keep her. It also means that Brandi is correct in being afraid because Julia will hunt her down. I myself have the same mark on my arm, a gift from Narcissismo. Most days I cover it up or apply makeup over it—the mark did not fit with my Mr. Nice story.

I clear my throat and push back the bitter memories of being sipped on repeatedly to the edge of death. "You may come with me to Arizona, then. But only until your family can safely retrieve you."

"Thank you, Racker." Without warning, she lunges forward, and I think she is going to attack, perhaps attempt to claw out my liver. Instead, she wraps her warm arms around my waist and buries her face in my chest, crying with the sort of vicious despair only someone like me could understand.

Slowly, my arm moves up to stroke her long soft hair. "There, there," I whisper, feeling oddly at peace offering her comfort. "All will be well."

An odd sense of ownership washes over me, but it is unlike what I felt with any of my human or vampire slaves in my past life. It is a sense of obligation I have never known. She is mine to care for and protect, for no other reason than I should. I want nothing in return.

What is happening to me? Maybe I am coming down with the flu.

CHAPTER SIX

Apparently, I have spent too much time in this modern human shell, and the supplements are beginning to affect my ancient mind. During the long drive back to Arizona, I noted water coming from the corners of my eyes each time I thought of returning to that big empty house, where I intend to rest, regroup, and re-strategize. No one on my list of allies will dare turn me now. Not until I prove I am still, and always will be, the notorious Mr. Nice. Ruthless, bloodthirsty, and all powerful.

The challenge is that I cannot provide the pudding until I am immortal.

"So whose house is this exactly?" Brandi asks as we pull up to the southwestern mansion situated in the Phoenix hills. The front yard is filled with a cactus garden that blooms with shades of hot pinks, reds, and oranges in the spring. The main part of the home is two stories tall with exposed wooden beams and large windows, modern but still very southwest.

"It belongs to friends," I say. "They are out of town. You will be safe here until your family comes for you." The home has a state-of-the-art security system, an iron fence around the perimeter, and a massive vault in the basement. Miriam, who was trained by her parents to kill vampires—a profession she turned away from obviously, considering her marriage choice—has an arsenal of weapons, too. Crossbows, knives, and chocolate-filled bullets. Chocolate is a narcotic for vampires. If Julia comes for us, we will have ample warning. We will be prepared.

Brandi's inquisitive eyes scan the impressive façade and tall fence as we drive through. "Must be some well-off friends."

I remain silent and park in the garage. I feel a bit foolish returning here, but out of the four hundred plus homes I own, none are fortresses. I never had the need for security as Mr. Nice.

I exit the car and head inside. "Hungry?" I say as Brandi follows.

"Yes."

"Too bad. Because I don't cook. Help yourself to whatever's in the fridge."

I head straight for the kitchen and grab a bowl, which I fill with cereal.

A warm hand stops me. "I make a mean steak. Or burger? If you have spaghetti, I can do that, too?"

Oh, how I miss spaghetti night. Miriam is an excellent cook. My mouth waters. "There is ground beef in the freezer."

"You got it." Brandi gets to work exploring the

cupboards in the kitchen—a modern space with a large gas stove and granite counters. "I'll get dinner going and then call my parents. May I use the phone?"

"Help yourself." I jerk my head toward the other room. "There is a landline in the study, just through that door. I will make up the guest room for you."

I go down the hallway to one of several rooms in the home. The guest suite is a small chamber, thirty by twenty with a private patio, jet tub, and king-sized bed. Nothing compared to the nursery with the full-sized gym and sauna, but what can I say? I suppose I am a mama's boy.

Was a mama's boy. I push back the memories lingering in every corner of this house, but then my mind drifts, wondering where they are now.

What are they doing?

Vacation in Greece?

Perhaps they rented a villa in Italy.

As a vampire, Michael is required to obtain a visa before entering another society's territory, so I am certain the office here in Arizona knows where they have gone. They would have assisted him with the paperwork.

No. I will not go and inquire. I do not care. They are gone.

I pull a clean set of sheets and a comforter from the closet so Brandi can make a fresh bed for herself. I check the bathroom to ensure there are supplies—

towels, shampoo, soap, toothbrush, toothpaste.

I will go upstairs and borrow some clothes from Miriam's closet. I am certain Brandi will want to wash the stench of Julia off her skin and wear something clean.

I enter the grand master bedroom upstairs and note the emptiness in the room. The bed looks like a grave where my memories are buried. Gone and buried.

So many good times in that bed. I loved when Vanderhorst would be in the mood and realize there was a crying infant in his spot. That look on his face when he knew he'd be spending yet another night with his hand in the shower. Alone.

Hehehe…

Afterward, he would come to bed and move me to the middle. I often unfastened my diaper and peed on him. He would lose his temper and accuse me of doing it on purpose, but Miriam would always come to my rescue. "You're letting the past get in your head. The old Nice is gone," she would say.

"I'm telling you, Miriam, he is a bad apple," Vanderhorst would argue.

"Don't say that. We are good people, and if he's raised right, he will be, too."

Looking back, Vanderhorst always knew what I was. He could smell my blood. So why didn't he send me away? Why not tell Miriam the truth?

I wonder if he did not wish to break her heart.

He knew how much she loved me. My mind drifts to the video she left. I have yet to hear it, and I miss the soothing sound of her voice.

I pull out my phone and tap on the message.

Miriam's red face comes into view. "Hello, Nice. I'm sure you've read the note Michael wrote, but knowing you, you've come up with some delusional story in your mind about why we left. I want to set the record straight, in case you have any thoughts about coming to look for us." She draws a slow breath and blots her puffy red eyes with a tissue. "We are leaving because if we don't, Michael will kill you. And as silly as it sounds, I still can't accept what's happened, that you would deceive me like that."

She shakes her head in disgust. "I mean, after I took the cure, I had no memory of you or Michael or Stella. In my mind, I was twenty. My parents were still alive and still furious with me for becoming a librarian and refusing to be a Keeper." The Keepers are a group of human vampire hunters her parents belonged to. "So when Michael showed up one day, imagine my shock when he told me everything that had happened—how you took me from him, how you turned me into a vampire against my will—but worst of all, I couldn't remember my own daughter. I lost the memory of her growing in my belly, of holding her and feeding her. All that was taken from me, Nice, because of you. Because of you and your games." Miriam straightens her spine. "But you know what? When Michael introduced me to the man who'd robbed me of everything, all I saw was a tiny, innocent baby. All I saw was a chance to get back something I'd lost. I decided then and there that the past was the past. I figured I had my daughter back, and I already felt a special connection with Michael. I knew with time, I would feel love for them again. But with you, I loved you from the first moment I held you." Miriam begins to break down, and I see Michael's arm reach for her shoulder from off-screen.

"That's enough, my love," he says. "You've said enough. Let us go now before he wakes."

"No, Michael. He needs to hear this." She looks at the camera. "I loved you like my own child, and you have stolen that from me. Again. It was all a game to you, and that is also why I'm leaving today. I never want to see you again. I never want to hear your name spoken until it comes accompanied by the news that you are dead. Goodbye."

She ends the video, and I feel a strange sensation in my chest, like it's caving in. Suddenly, there is moisture collecting in the corners of my eyes again.

I have lost her. My Miriam. All along I thought that somewhere deep inside her heart, she had feelings for me, that she would remember. But she only saw me as an opportunity to reclaim her lost years of motherhood with Stella.

It was motherly love all along.

The realization makes me feel surprisingly dirty

inside. What she felt was pure and unconditional despite our history. What I felt for her was quite the opposite.

"Racker? Hello!" I hear Brandi's voice down the hall.

"In here," I say, wiping my eyes to hide the evidence of my unexpected wimpy emotions.

Moments later, she pops her head in. "I was calling you from downstairs, but you didn't answer. I got worried."

Ah, yes. Brandi fears being alone. "All is well. As I said, this home is a fortress. If anyone attempts to get in, we will know."

She nods, but I sense my words do not ease her fears. "Well, um, the phone isn't working. I was wondering if I could use your cell again? I want to let my parents know I'm safe."

Brandi already called them from the road. It had been a brief but teary exchange. She told them she was all right and moving to a safe place where they could come get her.

"Of course."

I hand her the phone.

"Who's she?" Brandi asks.

I forgot to close out Miriam's video. "An old acquaintance."

Brandi stares at the screen. "This is her house. I saw a photo of her down in the study. She's with a man, a little girl, and she's holding a baby in a leather onesie."

I smile. The leather onesie was one of my ingenious methods of torturing Vanderhorst. It served to remind him who I really was. Psychological torture. I would cry for hours until they put it on me. Of course, the onesie wasn't made of real leather, but it did look rather nice. I was a badass, even as a baby.

"Yes, that baby would be yours truly."

Brandi frowns. "So those are your parents?"

"No. Not exactly. They raised me. This time, anyway." I begin telling Brandi the short version of the story, leaving out the part about being a notorious, evil vampire, feared by all.

"You're joking."

"Which part of my story do you find difficult to believe?" She already knows that vampires are real.

"So you took a cure, turned into a baby, and then your enemy raised you?"

"Yes, and his brother has prohibited anyone from turning me."

"But why would you want to be a vampire again? I just don't get it."

"Because I am experiencing a rare side effect of the cure, and that photo in the study was taken five years ago," I reply.

Brandi is a smart one. I know this because it takes her a mere two seconds to connect all the dots. "That's why you wanted Julia to turn you. And, ohmygod, I messed it up."

I nod.

She cups a hand over her mouth. "I'm so sorry.

I didn't know."

"What's done is done." I raise my chin.

"But you're sure no one's willing to turn you?"

"Yes." Any allies I had will turn their backs on me now.

"But can't we, I don't know, catch a vampire and force him to turn you?"

"Any vampire that weak would not be an adequate maker. I would be victimized by the stronger ones—mostly my friends."

"I'm sorry, but your vampire friends sound like a bunch of assholes," Brandi says.

"All the same, I would rather accept my fate and die than be turned by a watered-down, weakling, hundredth-generation vampire." The most respected vampires are powerful vampires. And to be powerful, you must have a close lineage to the original twelve vampires. Second-, third-, and fourth-generation vampires are very strong. Of course, vampires also grow stronger with age, but lineage trumps everything else.

Narcissismo was a fourth generation, which made me a five. Not good enough. I quickly came to realize that if I wanted power, I had to fake my way to the top. So I began convincing other vampires I was a second generation—a big step above most. I became quite good at demonstrating my speed, a skill I had to work hard at achieving.

After a while, I had everyone believing I was a force to be reckoned with. Of course, I actually was.

With so many allies and everyone fearing me, there has never been a more powerful vampire. Even Vanderhorst, the legendary Executioner, feared me.

"No wonder you look upset." Brandi sits down beside me. "I'm so sorry. Really. If there's anything I can do."

"I am afraid not."

"So what will happen? Where will you…" Her voice fades.

"Where will I age to death?" I shrug. "I had thought to go to Paris or Seville, but I now have the urge to die here."

"In Phoenix?"

"In this bed. I think it only appropriate to ruin it."

Brandi frowns. "You want to ruin your parents' bed?"

"It's complicated."

"Okay." She pats my leg. "I should get downstairs and check the sauce."

"I will find you some clean clothes and be down in a moment."

"Thanks again." She holds up my phone. "For everything, Racker."

I nod and watch her leave. I have thrown my life away to save one tiny mortal, who will be dead in sixty years.

Smart move, Nice.

At least she is enjoyable company. Not too hard on the eyes either. Perhaps knowing she will have the chance to live her dream—find love, get married, have a family—will ease my sense of stupidity.

I pause and give it some thought.

Nope.

CHAPTER SEVEN

I find several clean T-shirts, a few of those light stretchy sundresses Miriam likes to wear in this summer heat, a nightgown, and sweats for Brandi to wear until her family can come for her. I take a shortcut through the house and use the spiral staircase in the library to go downstairs. But as I descend, I begin thinking about all the books I have yet to read.

I do love reading. But even I, the once great Mr. Nice, hardly had time for it. I kept telling myself I had eternity to read them all, but now it dawns on me how mistaken I was.

Tonight, I will begin reading *The Lord of the Rings*. Then I will work my way through Harry Potter, *Game of Thrones*, and perhaps even Jane Austen—all of the contemporary works. After that Voltaire, Dante, and Nietzsche. Perhaps I will treat myself to another Mimi Jean book. They do make me laugh. Her depiction of vampires is ridiculous.

I was always surprised how much Miriam gushed over this *Fanged Love* series I pretended to enjoy so much. Vampires who are destined only to love one person? A mate? I've never heard anything so ridiculous. That's like saying there is only one sunrise for each person or only one pair of leather pants.

I enter the kitchen but do not find Brandi. Water is rapidly boiling on the stove, and a delicious-smelling tomato sauce is bubbling away in a saucepan. My mouth waters.

A murmur coming from the direction of the study catches my attention. I follow the sound and find Brandi looking out the window, pleading with someone on the phone.

"Dad, I promise I'm okay. It's a long story, but I'm safe."

Pause.

"No. I can't come home just yet. And I can't explain, so you'll have to trust me."

Brandi is telling her family not to come get her. Why would she do this?

She continues, "I will call you twice a day. And you have the address where I'm staying so you know where I am. I just need a few days before you come for me, all right? It's something I have to do."

I lean into the doorway and fold my arms over my chest.

"Bye, Mom. Bye, Dad. I love you. Say hi to Marigold for me." Brandi ends the call and turns, jumping out of her skin the moment she sees me. "Jesus! You scared me."

I cock a brow. "Mind telling me what you think you are doing?"

"Well, I-I'm not ready to face my family yet. I need to figure out how I'll explain what happened and that there's a vampire after me. I figured you wouldn't mind if I stayed a little longer. I hope that wasn't overreaching?"

"I thought that all you wanted was to see your family again."

"I do, but...I can't let them see me like this." She swipes a hand in front of her body.

Like what? Brandi looks rested and, well, generally lovely. Her brown eyes have a lively sparkle, her olive skin is smooth and creamy, and her dark hair shines like a new penny. She is a natural beauty in a curvy little package. I especially like how her chin dips in the middle. "You look perfectly fine after your ordeal."

"Ah, that would be the old Botellino genes in action." She swings her fist through the air. "Never let 'em see you sweat."

I rub my scruffy jaw, which is due for a shave. As a mortal, it is something I avoid. I loathe nicking myself. "So you wish to remain here and regroup."

She nods.

I do not believe her, but her motives don't concern me. "Make yourself at home, then. I placed some clean clothes in your room." I turn and head down the hallway toward the back stairs leading to my room, and she follows along.

"Where are you going? You haven't eaten yet."

"I have lost my appetite. Good night." I go to

my room and draw a hot bath. I have much to ponder, including the question that weighs heavily on my mind. When I am done reading the classics, do I truly wish to sit around waiting for death to come? After so many centuries of living a calculated life, perhaps I should end things on my own terms.

Or should I hold out hope that I will find a way through this?

Miracles are not for the evil. The evil get lucky from time to time, but God does not watch out for us. Vampires especially.

∂∾ ∾∫

The next morning, I wake to the smell of fresh coffee, warm bread, and bacon. I cannot help but feel my spirits lift. I march downstairs and find Brandi has prepared a feast of carbs.

Before, I would have shunned such a meal, but today I am all in. What does it matter if my body is not in tip-top shape? I am no longer worried about being frozen in time.

"Wow." I inspect the spread she has laid out. "Is this all for us?"

"You skipped dinner last night, so I thought you might be hungry?" She tosses a dish towel over her shoulder. "I made blueberry pancakes from scratch, scrambled eggs, biscuits, and the rest, well, you can see."

My mouth waters, and I take a seat. She serves

me a little of everything.

I take the first bite of pancake drowning in butter and maple syrup. It is like heaven. I try some of the coffee, rich and dark. *Like my librarian used to make.* "This is very nice of you, Brandi."

"Least I could do for the guy who saved my life."

Something I regret, but I do not tell her so. What is the point? What's done is done. I made my choice to exchange my life for hers.

"So, what's on the agenda for today?" she asks.

"I plan to spend some time reading. Thought I would stop by the library downtown first."

"But there are so many books in this house."

"The collection here lacks some of the modern works I wish to read. I will have to check those out." Actually, Miriam is gone. I will just take them. The keys to the library are in the drawer. "You may stay here. Rest assured you will be safe, and if anything should happen, I will only be twenty minutes away."

"Oh. Okay. But…I think I'd like to come with you."

"Brandi, you do not have to. I promise you will be safe. Otherwise, I would not have brought you here."

She takes a tiny bite of a biscuit she's slathered with butter and honey. For a second, I am mesmerized by the action. She has such lovely lips. I wonder what her mouth would look like with a set of shiny white fangs. *Hot.*

"Why are you looking at me like that?" she asks.

"I think I see why Julia wished to enslave you."

Brandi's smile melts away into a dreary look. She slides a hand over her breast, over the spot where she has been marked.

"You do not need to feel ashamed, woman."

"Excuse me?" Brandi arches a dark brow.

"No need to feel ashamed." Did she not hear me?

"You think I'm ashamed?"

"No?" I question.

"No. I'm angry. That monster had no right to take me. She had no right to mark my skin like that."

"She had every right," I say flatly. "In her mind, anyway. Vampires are at the top of the food chain, and you were merely a thing, an object she wished to own."

"Well, that's just...fucked up."

"It is the way of the world. One species dominates another, and if you have doubts, I urge you to look down at your plate. Oink. Oink," I say dryly.

Her brown eyes drift toward the crispy strip of bacon next to her scrambled eggs.

"Everything must eat, Brandi. The animal kingdom is called so for a reason. Because we are all animals. Not saints. Not angels."

"But—but—humans don't taunt our food. We don't bite them and tattoo their nipples with bats!" She pounds her fist on the table.

"Tell that to the cow marked with a branding iron."

She narrows her eyes. "I'm not saying that humans can't be cruel. We know they're capable of brutality. And yes, we eat meat. But I don't know many people who sit around salivating over watching an animal cry in pain."

I shrug. "You think the cow cares whether or not you're entertained by its death? All it knows is that it is not free, that it is about to die, and that there is nothing it can do about it."

Brandi narrows her eyes. "So you're basically saying I'm no different than Julia?"

I stare and say nothing. She knows the answer.

Brandi stands, nostrils flaring. "I see it now. I can tell you really were a vampire once."

"What does that mean?"

"It means that you think it's your right to mistreat anything weaker than you, that the fact you've been given a soul and mind, capable of distinguishing cruelty from simple survival, means nothing." She exhales. "In reality, though, you're the cow. You're trapped."

I scoff. "How so, woman?"

"Because you don't see you've been given a gift. You don't have to accept being anything you don't want to be."

"I have been alive for over three hundred years, Brandi. So, while I applaud your valiant effort to enlighten me about the fine art of breaking molds, you are out of your depth. I have reinvented myself so many times, I cannot recall all of the faces I've worn."

"And yet you still don't know who you are." She points to herself. "But I sure as hell do. So figure that one out, Racker."

She marches from the kitchen, leaving me to stew in the juices of her words. "I know who I am! Thank you very much, human!" *I am a vampire man! Vampire on the inside. Man on the outside.*

But as I say the words, my mind fills with heavy thoughts. Yes, I know who I am, but so what? I am stuck in a body that will soon die, and I wonder what's been the point of this long, long life if it's all led to this moment. I have wasted my entire existence, planning for something that will never happen. No world domination. Had I known, I could have been out there, enjoying my life. Living instead of dreaming.

I tilt my head toward the ceiling. If I somehow get out of this, I vow not to waste another moment on such ridiculous goals. I will live life to its fullest.

CHAPTER EIGHT

Later that morning, I shower and dress in a low-effort outfit. Jeans, black T-shirt, biker boots. I barely had the energy to condition my wavy locks but somehow muscled through the task. Mostly because I know the days are numbered for us. Soon I will find clumps of shiny strands on my pillow when I wake.

I get in the SUV and start the engine. *Day one of the last year of my life.* I will make the most of it.

"Hey." Brandi slides into the passenger seat, dressed in a peach-colored sundress that makes her skin look more golden brown than olive. Her long hair is in a high ponytail, exposing her long neck, and she's wearing a pair of flip-flops we have for guest use around the pool. Her cute little toes are sticking out, the nails painted pale pink.

I stare at her inquisitively. She looks adorable, which is entirely inappropriate. I'm on a quest to fulfill my final wish before I die. *Could she at least try to look less picnicky and cute?*

"What?" she asks.

"Nothing." I am not in the mood to quarrel again. If she wishes to come along dressed like that, then fine.

I hit the road and take us to the library that has become like a second home to me. Miriam's parents founded this place, likely as a justification for their book-collecting addiction—something passed down for several generations. Her parents hadn't expected her to make the library her calling, but she did. I think it was something I admired about her. She chose a path different from what others demanded of her.

"So your mom is the librarian here?" Brandi asks as we park in the lot. Oddly, there are several other cars here.

"My mother died long ago." True. But really I do not wish to hear Miriam referred to that way. Not anymore.

"All right then. So the woman who took care of you these past five years is the librarian here?"

"Something like that," I grumble.

"I love my family, so don't get me wrong, but you kinda hit the lottery with your adoptive family." Brandi hops from the SUV. "They sound pretty cool."

"Sure. Cool." I shut off the engine, get out, and dig for the library key in my jeans pocket. When I get to the door, Brandi is already on her way inside. I spot a woman waiting next to the empty checkout counter.

Hold on. Miriam is on "vacation" for a year. Who let people in?

"I'll be over in the travel section." Brandi turns for a nearby aisle, almost getting run over by a tall blonde with a huge bun atop her head. She's wearing the chunkiest glasses I've ever seen.

"Oh, pardon me," says the blonde.

Brandi gives her a quick nod, flashes a strange look my way, and then disappears.

The blonde glances at me, too, and then heads behind the counter, where she hands a book to the waiting woman. "All right, sweetie pie! Here is your book. It's due back next Wednesday. Now don't you forget, 'kay?"

"Tell Miriam I hope she enjoys her time off," the woman says, "but we want to see her back soon for those awesome story times."

Wondering what's going on, I stare at the blonde. Her sweater is three sizes too large, and she looks like she applied her pink lipstick while four-wheel driving on the moon.

Yum… The nerdy mess before me is so over-the-top sexy that my heart stops beating for two entire seconds. I love the hot bookworm look. It's right up there with naughty nurses.

Suddenly, her hand moves lightning fast to scratch her nose.

Gasp! She's a vampire.

I wait until she is alone and walk up to the counter. "Who are you?" I whisper.

"Sorry, sir?" she says with a chipper tone.

"I know what you are, but not *who* or why

you're here when Miriam is out of town."

"Oh. Well, Miriam and Michael are friends with my aunt Myrtle. They asked her to help out with the library for a few months, but something came up at the last minute, so my aunt asked me to come."

Aunt, huh? She means one of her coven friends, possibly. "So which society do you belong to?"

"I'm sorry, sir, but I don't believe we are acquainted. You are?"

I love that she's pretending to have no clue who I am. "Nice."

She giggles. "Aren't we all. And even if we aren't, who would admit to it?"

I frown. "Me. I would."

"Ha! You're funny. Well, I'm Liza."

I nod, trying to puzzle her out. "And you have no idea who I am?"

"No. Should I?"

"It is simply that I…" I am about to say that I am a notorious vampire, but if she doesn't know me, this could be the miracle I've been hoping for. Is it possible there is a vampire in the world who has never heard my name?

"You are…?" She arches a blonde brow.

"The name is Racker. And I am familiar with your kind." I lift the sleeve of my shirt to show the black bat tattoo on my bicep.

"Oh!" Her blue eyes go wide. "Wow. I never would have guessed it."

"Why?"

"Well, the way you came in and just spoke to me. Very confident. You don't strike me as," she lowers her voice, "a human slave."

"That is because I am not. Not any longer." I lift my chin.

"Ah! A free bird. Congratulations. I never liked that practice. It's forbidden by law, anyway."

"True, but laws are really more like just guidelines when it comes to our—I mean, *your* kind."

"I suppose."

"So which society are you from?" I repeat. She has never heard my name, so it must be somewhere remote.

"I am what you would call a nomad. *Sans société.* I've been living as a yak herder in the Himalayas for the last few decades. Before that, I spent time on this really weird island in the Bahamas with this monk named Mr. Rook, who…"

As Liza goes on for the next ten minutes about all the places she's lived, it becomes abundantly clear that she has been off the grid longer than I have been alive. Is it possible that this female vampire is older than Narcissismo?

"So you are an ancient powerful vampire, then?" I ask, practically salivating at the thought of someone like her turning me. In the vampire world, the pecking order is heavily dependent on who made who and how pure their blood is.

"We're all equally powerful in my eyes, part of

one big universe. Vampire. Human. Yak. Are we really so different at the end of the day?"

An ancient vampire can kill a hundred human men in sixty seconds, while a yak might do what? Nibble on your hair? Hardly equal.

"But you must be at least a third or a fourth generation. Correct?" I ask. Not that it matters which. As long as she is of superior strength compared to most vampires, she will do.

"Technically, I'm a second generation."

What! Someone pinch me! Or better yet, someone bite me.

She continues, "My maker was a huge macho jerk. Only made female vampires because he thought we would serve him. Finally, everyone in our coven got sick of his whole ass grabbing and chauvinistic talk—" she lowers her voice, pretending to talk like a man "—female vampires are meant to live in caves, barefoot, waiting to please their maker with a warm human on the table when he comes home." Liza exhales and smiles proudly. "So we shared his blood and dusted him."

She is saying that they devoured the vampire who created them. And, as every vampire knows, if one ingests the blood of a stronger vampire, they inherit their powers. Sounds a bit confusing, unless you're a virologist with a background in genetic mutations. In short, vampirism is caused by an ancient virus.

The original strain is the most powerful, though

no one knows its origin. As the virus is passed down from vampire to vampire, the strain weakens. All that sciency stuff aside, I cannot believe my luck. She will be the perfect maker for me! "So you are essentially here for a vacation?"

Liza giggles. "Not exactly."

"Then?"

"Well, I think it's finally time to set down roots. I've seen it all, done it all. Everything except the one. The big L."

Love. She wants love. *She is perfect!*

"I am sure you will find it, Liza. A woman such as yourself…" I reach for her hand and kiss the top. "…will have no issues finding suitors." I gaze into her azure blue eyes. "But how will you ever choose? I'm sure the gentlemen are lined up around the block."

She snorts and jerks her hand away. "Well, yan-no. I guess a lottery would be the fairest." She doubles over and laughs hysterically, snorting profusely.

It takes everything I have not to show what I am thinking: *What the hell is the matter with this one?*

Still, one cannot look a gift horse in the mouth. She is attractive and physically stirs me in all the right places. Check that box.

She is an ancient vampire. Check that box, too.

And, most importantly, she seems to have no clue who I am. *Check, check, check!*

"Liza, since you're new in town, why don't I

take you to dinner tonight? I can show you a place that makes a mean Mongolian beef. Very spicy." Vampires love hot food.

"Oh. Ohhhh. Sounds good."

"Then I shall see you around eight?" I say.

"Sounds great." She smiles, flashing a bit of sexy fang.

"And where should I retrieve you from?"

She gives me the address of her rental. It is not far from the library. "See you then. And please wear something breathable."

"Sorry?" she says.

"It's going to be a hot night." I wink.

She stares blankly.

"The restaurant has the hottest peppers in town. You will be sweating."

"Oh." She swipes a hand through the air. "Very funny!"

I saunter out to await Brandi in the car. I have forgotten all about reading myself to death or dying of old age. Liza is quite possibly the sexiest woman I have encountered in my existence. She gets my vampire juices flowing, which says a lot! I have no vampire juice.

"Racker?" says a soft voice.

I turn my head and find Brandi sitting next to me in the passenger seat. I hadn't even noticed her getting into the car.

"You're really going out with her? Tonight?"

"You heard all that?" I ask.

"Yes. And I know what she is."

"How?"

"After what I went through, a person just knows," Brandi growls her words.

"What has your panties in a brunch, woman?"

"It's bunch."

I shrug. "Who cares? I don't wear panties, now do I?" I wait for her to disclose what's eating her. "Well? Out with it."

Her warm brown eyes flicker with anger. Her pouty little lips are puckered in an angry little circle. "Never mind. Can we go now?"

"Yes, but you must help me prepare for this date."

"Why do you want my help?"

"Because you are a woman, and I must practice my game."

"Game?" Brandi frowns.

"Liza does not know who I am, and she thinks I have always been human. I must practice behaving like a modern man while wooing her at the same time."

"Why not just tell her the truth?"

Brandi clearly doesn't understand the complexities of my situation. "Because she is my last chance at becoming a vampire again."

Brandi runs her petite hands over the length of her ponytail. "You're serious. You really plan to seduce her so she'll turn you."

"She is quite beautiful. I wouldn't mind bedding her too." I always preferred sleeping with vampires. I like it rough. I like to push boundaries. And I go for hours. A human could never keep up.

Brandi shakes her head. She doesn't approve.

"So you are refusing to help me? The man who nearly died rescuing you from a vicious vampire, therefore tarnishing my three-century-old reputation in the vampire world."

"You're not playing fair."

"Judge me if you like, but you owe me," I add.

"Fine. I'll help. But promise me, if this works, you won't end up being like that monster Julia."

She is a reproachable specimen. Even at my worst, I would never have kept my house looking like that. "You have my word."

CHAPTER NINE

Liza. Liza. Liza! Words cannot express the joy I feel tonight. To think, there is an ancient vampire out there who has no clue I am Mr. Nice. It's like winning the lottery. She is also beautiful, well traveled, and had no issues accepting an invitation from a human male with the mark of the bat.

"It is almost too good to be true." I check my hair one final time in the foyer mirror.

"Just remember what I told you, okay?" says Brandi, already prepared for bed in sweats and a T-shirt. "Talk about her. Ask questions about what she likes, her travels, any hobbies. If a topic makes her eyes light up, ask more questions about that. If she asks about you or your past, just sidestep and say something vague, like, her life sounds way more interesting. But don't be pushy! Let the conversation flow naturally and, repeat after me, I will not showboat. I will not showboat."

I nod. Brandi and I spent the afternoon practicing the fine art of modern human conversation. I can converse just fine as a vampire, but I'm supposed to be human. One hundred percent.

My biggest challenge will be pretending I do not

know as much as I do. I too am well traveled, well educated, and well lived. Luckily, I have spent most of my existence playing a role. "Got it. How do I look?"

"Like you're about to fight a bull."

Brandi does not support my red cape.

"Woman! What do you want from me? I am in jeans. And I have put on one of these hideous pastel pink button-down shirts you insist I wear. What more do you want?"

She backs away, holding up her hands. "Just trying to help. I don't want you to die of old age because of your fashion choices. But what do I care?" She says that last part with a bitter edge, like I'm a moron for not seeing how vested she is in my plight.

"Funny."

Her eyes whip to mine. "How's that funny?"

"You've known me all of two days."

"So?"

"You expect me to believe that you genuinely care for my well-being? We hardly know each other."

She looks like she wants to claw out my eyes. "Did you actually put me down just now because I showed concern for you?" She shakes her head. "You're damaged."

I feel my conscience kick in. I am extremely un-trusting, and I know it. Comes with the territory of living among my kind for three centuries.

"Apologies. I was out of line." I remove the cape and toss it to the bench next to the door. "I am nervous. Can you imagine? Me. I have never been nervous in my life."

"Just promise, if you convince her to change you, that you won't become a turd like Julia."

This is the second time she's mentioned that. I don't understand where this is coming from, but, all right, "Yes. Fine. I promise."

"Just making sure. Have a great date." She marches to her room and slams the door.

What has gotten under her skin? "I turned on the hot tub! Maybe you need to soak away that nasty attitude, young lady!"

I don't have a clue why she is behaving so oddly, but I cannot afford to lose focus. Everything is riding on tonight. I must win Liza over, at least enough to get some of her blood. If I am lucky, she will do it while we are in the throes of passion.

༄ ༄

"You're a virgin?" From a quiet corner of my favorite Chinese restaurant, I gaze across the table at Liza over a steaming plate of spicy onions and eggplant. The establishment is a hole-in-the-wall with old carpets and too much dust on the dragon-painted lamps. Still, there is no better food in town. *And no better view.*

Liza looks stunning tonight with her huge

blonde bun, thick glasses and a bulky dress that resembles a floral potato sack. I really appreciate when a woman is confident in herself and doesn't try to impress. Her look says 'I am sexy underneath this wall of impenetrable fabric. But you won't get to see it unless you impress me first.'

"Yes, well," she says, "I was raised by a very strict family in a small village. Women were expected to save themselves for marriage, and I guess after I was turned, I never really let go of my traditional upbringing."

"But you are very old. That is a long time to wait."

She plucks a piece of eggplant from the plate and pops it in her mouth. Meanwhile, my eyes are tearing from the fumes. There is an inch of fire-roasted hot peppers on the dish—special order. The waitress looked at us like we were mad. Even now, I keep seeing the chef poke his head out from the kitchen. He cannot believe we are eating it.

"Oh, trust me," she says. "I wasn't waiting. I was too busy living. One adventure after another until one day, boom! Five hundred years went by. It's been an amazing journey."

I am almost jealous. Liza has been taking in all the experiences life has to offer, while I spent my years acquiring wealth and power. Look where that got me. I still have the money, but I am about as powerful as a three-legged caterpillar. "So now you're here in Phoenix, looking after Miriam's library."

"Just until my aunt comes. Then I'm off again."

"To where?"

"Not sure. But it's time, yanno? Sex and love are the two things I've yet to experience. Well, that and having children."

"Children? You mean, you wish to turn someone?"

She laughs and waves a dismissive hand through the air. "God no. I've never given anyone my blood. Don't plan to either. I mean, it would have to be a very special person under very special circumstances—someone I really trust and love. But I meant real children. I plan to take the cure and have actual babies."

My throat goes dry. "Babies? The cure?"

"Yeah, there's a cure now. It took a while for them to get the dosage right, but they can reverse vampirism. Isn't that wonderful?"

I know all too well about the cure. *Ground zero here.* "I have heard of this cure—through my vampire friends, of course. They mentioned there is an issue with memory loss." I am one of the only known exceptions. It's a miracle that Vanderhorst did not lock me up in the lab for further study. No memory loss, an extreme age makeover, and rapid aging. They assume there was a reaction to the large dose I consumed, but no one truly knows for certain.

"My entire existence as a vampire will be erased

from my mind," she says. "When I wake up, there'll be a new life waiting for me, which is why I have to make preparations. I'm thinking of recording a few videos for myself to explain why I'm no longer living in the 1500s. I kind of hoped to meet my special someone first, so I have help adjusting to what will seem like an entirely new world, but after some thought, I decided not to wait. I'm going for it." She shrugs. "Mr. Right will come along when he does. Plus, I figure it'll be easier to meet a human guy if I'm human, too."

This is a disaster. My savior intends to become human again. Soon. And she wants a human companion. "Not to put a damper on your dreams, Liza, but have you ever considered that your soul mate might be like you?"

She blinks.

I continue, "And forgive me for being so frank, since we hardly know each other, but you are one of the most well-adjusted, eh hem—" I do not want to say *vampire* out loud in a public place "—persons of your kind I have ever met. I think you were born for it."

The waitress comes and delivers a plate of piping hot Mongolian beef with the tiniest chili peppers I've ever seen. I know they must be hot.

Liza's eyes light up. "That looks yummy. Dig in."

Not wanting to be rude, I grab my spoon and load some onto my plate. My tongue is still on fire from the eggplant I sampled.

I take a bite and feign a smile. "Yumm…" *Dear God, I am going to burst into flames. The pain! The pain!* "Really spectacular." I reach for my water and guzzle while Liza helps herself to the hellfire on our table.

"Wow. That *is* good. I've really missed meat. I've been living off yak herders and cheese for years."

"So," I try not to cry, "what do you think?"

"About?"

"Well, what if your Mr. Right is a vampire? Or is a human who wants to become one? It wouldn't be absurd for a man to want to spend eternity with a woman such as yourself. One human lifetime wouldn't be enough. At least, it wouldn't be for me if *I* truly loved a woman."

"Wow. Aren't you full of opinions?"

"I'm sorry. I merely meant to provoke a conversation. A habit of mine. I like to philosophize and debate." A lie. I am not in the habit of caring what others think.

"No. No. Don't apologize. I like people who make me think."

Good, because clearly you're not accustomed to doing it on your own. I mean, take the cure? Become human and weak again? She is mad!

She continues, "And maybe you're right. I've been so fixated on my plan that I forgot my motto: Go with the flow. My best adventures have always come from the most unexpected places."

"So you changed your mind? You are not taking the cure?" That was easy.

"I still plan to take it. I already have my date set. But if Mr. Right happened to have different thoughts on what species we should be, I'd definitely keep an open mind."

At least the door is still open to persuade her, but I do not have much time.

We spend the rest of dinner talking about her time living in the Amazonian jungle, traveling Asia on horseback, and living in an abandoned temple after taking a vow of silence that lasted several decades. All of which sounds extremely boring. Yes, I respect her for living her dreams, but wouldn't it have been more exciting to, I don't know, be around other living creatures? Converse with someone other than a rock? It seems like she did everything possible to avoid contact with humans and vampires alike.

I wonder why.

The answer might help me understand what makes her tick. One thing is clear, though, if she is looking for Mr. Right, I am not him.

But can I convince her I am? Because reading between the lines, it sounds like she'll do anything for love. Including turning them into a vampire.

CHAPTER TEN

"No, Racker. You can't do that. It's not right," Brandi protests from the comfort of the hot tub outside. I am pleased she decided to relax, but why does she think she has the right to judge me?

"I did not ask for your opinion." I fold my arms over my chest.

"Then why are you telling me?" she bites back.

Good question. I came home from my date filled with many questions, so I shared everything with Brandi, including Liza's plan to take the cure, find Mr. Right, and have babies. *Blech!* Then I asked Brandi what she thought would be the best way to convince Liza to change her plans so she'll turn me. *Boom! Guilt trip.*

"I told you," I say, "not because I seek your approval; I want your help. I have another date with Liza tomorrow."

"You seem to have everything under control." She sinks deeper into the water and looks away.

I push off my dress shoes, unbutton my hideous pink shirt, and slide off my jeans.

"What are you-you doing?" Brandi asks.

"Getting in the water."

"Naked? You're coming in naked?" she asks.

She averts her eyes, but only after taking in an eyeful, including my generous manhood. I do not care. Nudity is not something I have ever shied away from. Basically, vampires are big old nudists.

"I am not about to go in with my jeans on." I get into the water across from her. The heat and bubbles are just what I needed.

"Don't you own a swimsuit?" she grumbles.

"Are you wearing one?"

"Well, no, but that's because I was here alone, and I don't have one with me."

"Ah, but that is not the point. You are naked. I am naked. What is the problem?" Suddenly it dawns on me. We are naked. Together.

Nope. Nope. I do not like human women. I have never been with one, but that changes nothing. My taste in the bedroom is something a mortal female wouldn't enjoy. Lots of hard foreplay, maybe some spanking, and hours of pounding.

"Why are you looking at me like that?" Brandi asks.

"Like what?"

"Like you're eyeing a piece of chocolate cake." She crosses her arms over her chest, even though I can't see a thing. It's dark out, and there are tons of bubbles.

A shame. I would not mind looking at her breasts again. I am a male, after all, and the female form is one of the nicest things on the planet to look at.

"Do not be alarmed. I was merely trying to picture you naked in my bed, on all fours, taking my large co—"

"Whoa. Excuse me?" She holds up her palm.

"I do not wish to do that do you. I was simply trying to visualize what it would be like to sleep with a human woman, and you happened to be the one who popped in my mind. You're sitting right across from me. Don't read too much into it."

"So you've never been with a woman?" she asks.

"I have been with plenty, but they were all vampires."

"So you haven't…I mean…you haven't done it in that body?"

I shake my head. "No. Why? What am I missing out on? Don't all the parts fit together in the same way?"

"I guess so." She shrugs.

"Then?" She has piqued my curiosity with her inquiry.

"I imagine it would be, I don't know, nicer?"

"I have had plenty of *nice* sex." *Mr. Nice here.*

"No, I meant—vampires aren't exactly the warmest and friendliest of creatures."

"That is where you would be mistaken," I say, throwing back my head to let the jets work on my back muscles. "To a vampire male, there is nothing more sacred and alluring than his woman. He would take great care to please her in the most passionate of ways in the bedroom. Long massages, hours of oral pleasure, perhaps a finger in her bu—"

"Got it, thank you." Brandi looks away.

"There. You see. That is exactly why I have never been with a human woman. They are too shy. I like a woman who is unafraid to ask for what she wants. She must be completely open to all forms of pleasure and bodily exploration—nipples licked and teased and—"

"I get the idea. Thank you…"

I laugh. "My, my. Are you blushing, Brandi?" Even with the faint light coming from the pool, I can see her face is flushed.

"It's just the heat."

"Nope. I do believe your cheeks are flushed. Tell me, was it the word nipple?" I tease. "How about when I say cock?"

"Stop it, okay?"

"Are you shy, my little Brandi?" I chuckle. It is quite charming. Vampire women are never shy.

"So what? It's not a sin to be shy. And before you ask, I've actually never been with anyone. I'm saving myself for marriage. Also not a sin."

What is with all the virgins today? Is there an epidemic I am unaware of? "You've never known the pleasure of a man? Aren't you a little old to still be waiting?" I ask, but then wish to recant. I just met a five-hundred-year-old virgin. *That's old!*

"I'm only twenty-four."

I stare, brows raised.

"Fine," she grumbles. "By today's standards, it's uncommon to wait, but my parents are pretty traditional, and I guess I hate the thought of disappointing them."

"It is none of my business, but you are a grown woman. Your sex life is your business. They should not be involved."

She floats her small hands on the surface of the water, staring at the bubbles. "My parents aren't involved. They just have expectations. They work hard and want my sister and me to live honest, wholesome, purposeful lives. It's why I'm getting my graduate degree in English, to be a teacher."

"You do not *wish* to teach?"

"No. I mean, yes. I want them to be proud."

Brandi would never make it as a vampire. Self-ishness is the name of the game. "That is not the same as *you* wanting it, and though this will sound odd coming from a three-hundred-year-old ex-vampire, life is short. You must seize the day. What is it you wish to do with your life?"

"I don't know." She groans and scrubs her face with her wet hands.

"You must have some passions or interests?" Knitting, cooking, cleaning? You know, women's work.

"I guess…I always pictured being what they wanted me to be. I love them, and to me that always meant making them happy."

This is the exact opposite of my philosophy in

life. *Serve thyself first.* Because no one else really gives a crap about you.

Nevertheless, I find her desire to make her family proud to be amiable. "Well, I am certain they would love that you're staying with me, then." I pretend to polish my nails on my chest.

Brandi chuckles. "They'd send me to an exorcist."

"I hope not. Demons love exorcists, and I doubt you'd find the evil bastards good company." Frankly, I never understood why humans send possessed individuals to the very people who are surrounded by demons.

"Demons are real?" Her eyes go wide.

"Do not worry, unless you're hanging out with priests, you are safe."

"I'm hanging out with an ex-vampire. Where does that land on the scale of safe?" she asks.

"You cannot get any safer. I do not drink blood, and I know all of the vampires' tricks. I invented them." I also know the ins and outs of vampire politics. I was a territory leader for many years. One could say I am the only vampire alive who truly understands both vampire worlds—the seedy side and the goody-goody side.

Brandi smiles, but it is more of a glow that lights up her entire face. That image of her in my bedroom flashes in my head again, and I find myself stirring beneath the bubbles.

Suddenly, there is a tightness in my chest, followed by shooting pain.

"Racker? Racker! Are you okay?" Brandi pushes up out of the water and grabs hold of my shoulders.

"My chest. It hurts." I groan, pressing my fist over my heart.

"Christ, I think you're having a heart attack."

She hops from the water and pulls me out. If I weren't in so much pain, I would be commenting on her shocking strength. She rolls me onto the patio. "Don't move. I'm going to call an ambulance."

"No…" I groan. "No ambulance."

"You need medical attention."

"Can't. Afford. To lose. Time," I mumble.

Brandi is smart. She must understand why. They would start running tests and see something is very different about me. Aside from my impressive manhood and incredible body, I mean. "Then what do I do?"

My chest gets tighter. "Can't breathe…"

"Oh God. No, no, no. Don't die." She leans over me and starts mouth-to-mouth.

I'm only vaguely aware of her warm, wet, bare breasts pressed to my chest, but it's enough to know her skin feels good on mine. So soft. And her lips are silky and smooth. Gentle yet firm.

Bad, very bad. The blood in my body starts flowing the wrong way. "Worse. Making it worse."

"What?" She kneels beside me. "What are you saying?"

"More…"

"I thought you said stop." She leans over me again and presses her mouth to mine. Her naked breasts return to my chest, and I start to wonder what she might feel like if she were beneath me, breathing heavily in my ear, panting my name.

The pain begins to subside, replaced by something else. A deep, carnal warmth in my groin.

"Enough." I place my hand on her shoulder. I feel light-headed and, frankly, confused. "It has passed."

"So fast? Are you sure?" She pushes her damp hair off her forehead.

I sit up and note a burning sensation in my throat, followed by a burp. "I think it was my meal."

"What the hell did you eat?" She starts rubbing her lips like they're on fire.

"An obscene amount of very hot chili peppers." My eyes drift from her eyes down to her body. With the gentle light of the nearby pool, I note her supple round breasts, the narrow waist, and a patch of dark hair between her legs. She is very beautiful. Curves and smooth skin. She has the type of body artists would have killed to paint back in my human days. First human days. Even now, such a classic female form evokes thoughts of lust and urges of procreation. Her wide hips are a calling card for all things carnal.

Brandi realizes I am studying her female form.

"Stop. Look away."

"Why?"

"Because I asked you to."

"Fine. But you have nothing to be ashamed of. You are lovely." I turn my head, and she goes to grab her towel on the lounge chair.

I take a quick look at her tan round ass as she covers up.

"Not bad. For a human," I say under my breath.

"I'm going inside." She heads for the house, and I cannot help watching her leave. I like the way she walks—the sway in her hips, the sure stride, the feminine form of her body.

"Not bad yourself," she mutters as she disappears.

I smile. It is a shame that she is not a vampire. Otherwise, she would make a very nice companion. As is though, with my current rate of aging, I will be in my fifties within six months. Six months after that, I will be pushing ninety. This story ends one of two ways. Vampire or dead. And Brandi does not factor into either equation, even if I feel a sense of…of something toward her.

CHAPTER ELEVEN

The next morning, from the antique oak breakfast table, Brandi informs me that her parents are on their way from Missouri to retrieve her. They will arrive in less than two days' time.

I hate to admit it, but I will miss her and that sassy little mouth. I am beginning to think of her as a true friend. Everyone else knew me as Narcissismo's slave, Mr. Nice, or more recently, a very evil, but adorable infant. My parents knew me as Steviuus, the dutiful brave son, but that was so long ago. I recall very little of that person. For better or worse, Brandi knows the real me. It is almost liberating not to have to constantly pretend to be someone else around her. Her cooking isn't half bad either.

"I think you have outdone yourself, woman. These blueberry pancakes are amazing. A man could get used to eating like this."

"Thanks." She stares down at her plate and picks away at her fruit. I notice she did the same yesterday too—cooks up a storm but barely eats. The Julia situation must weigh heavily on her mind.

"You know, I was thinking, if I am successful

with Liza, that only solves one of our problems."

"Oh?" She doesn't seem to be paying attention.

"You have always dreamed of being a leprechaun, and I can make that happen. Pot of gold, green suit, and everything."

"Cool." She pokes a blueberry, then stares out the window at the backyard. It is another miserably sunny day, complete with chirping birds and an endless blue sky. *Blech!*

"All right. What's troubling you now?" I ask.

"Sorry?" She looks across the table at me with her tired eyes.

"What is the matter?"

"I didn't sleep much last night. Or the night before."

Ah yes. "That is what I was attempting to get at."

"What?"

"Your situation. After I am turned, I can take care of Julia for you. I will ensure you live in peace."

Brandi stares across the breakfast table. "That's really nice of you."

Actually, it's the opposite of Nice. *He would not have lifted a finger for you.* "It is the least I can do after you saved me. A very risky but brave move."

Brandi's chest rises high and falls fast with a heave.

"Are you not relieved?" I ask.

"I am."

But she still looks troubled—scrunched brows,

the corners of her pouty lips turned down.

"Say it. What else is bothering you?"

"Everything, actually. I'm angry Julia took me. I'm angry you had to give up so much to save me. I'm furious that a vampire threatened my family, and now I'm being hunted." She lets out a long groan. "I have no idea what I'm going to do."

"I already told you, I will take care of Julia."

"Let's get real, hero man. That's only if you manage to get turned, and even then, how are you going to find her before she finds me?"

I see her point.

Brandi continues, "I just don't know what I'll tell my family about all this. 'Hey, guys! I was kidnapped by a vampire, and now she's coming for us!'"

"Then lie."

"I wasn't raised like that."

Just like she was raised to save herself for marriage and follow a career simply to appease her parents? "I never pictured you as a poster child for obedience and piety."

"I have no idea what you're saying right now," she replies.

"It's simple. You think lying is wrong, sex is wrong, and putting your needs first is wrong. I would argue that the universe gave you free will for a reason. Sometimes we must lie to protect others and ourselves. Sometimes we have sex because we need to connect with another or we'll go mad.

Sometimes we follow a path in life, even if it upsets others, because it is our destiny."

"Are you saying I'm a coward?" Her lips mash into an angry flat line.

"No. From the moment I met you, I saw you for who you really are. A fighter. I think that is how you convinced me to do what I did. I, too, am a fighter." The tattoo on my arm is proof. I have only met thirteen individuals in my existence with such a mark. They are all dead with the exception of Brandi and myself. Human slaves are usually disposed of once they are no longer useful to their vampire master. "But to answer your question, I know you are lying about the real reason you wished to stay a bit longer, and I am trying to tell you not to be ashamed for acting in your own self-interest."

"What reason do you think that is?"

"With me, you feel free." I only realized it now because I feel the same way with her.

She stands from the table. "That isn't why I wanted to stay, you…you…dumbass."

I set down my fork and fold my arms over my chest. "Very well then. Enlighten me."

She blinks her expressive brown eyes. "Well-well, it's my fault your plans were messed up. Didn't feel right to bail on you like that."

"So," I say, my voice condescending, "you are here because you are worried about my immortal quest. So then why are you leaving now? My quest isn't over."

"Because I don't want to watch you play Liza. It's wrong."

I shrug. "One must do what's necessary to survive."

"No!" Brandi's little nostrils flare, and her cheeks turn red. "One must do what's right."

I stand from the breakfast table. "And according to you, what is that? Die before I'm ready? Grow old in this big house alone?"

"I don't have the answers, but I know you can't lie and hijack someone else's life, their happiness, for your own. *You* get to live the life that's given to *you*." She sighs. "That's it. You take the punches with the wins."

She stares at my lips, and I find myself staring at hers.

"And what sort of wins are you looking for?" I ask.

She says nothing. I'm suddenly thinking about grabbing her and "winning" with her on the table. I'm thinking about putting my mouth on her neck and kissing my way south. I love pushing boundaries, and with her, everything is a boundary.

Before I can process what's happening, I'm stepping around the table, about to go for it.

Wait. What am I doing? She is a virgin, and I am not about to change that. Not that there's anything wrong with taking what I want, as a vampire should, but it simply wouldn't feel right.

I must focus my energies on Liza, not on a

dead-end relationship. *Dead* being what will happen to me if I fail at convincing Liza to turn me.

"I, uh…must prepare for my workout. Thank you for breakfast." I turn and leave the kitchen, my body aflame with adrenaline. I need to relieve myself of these urges before I do something foolish.

I grab my bottle of lotion and head to my bathroom for a different sort of workout.

I avoid Brandi for the remainder of the day, and I know what you all must be thinking: I am growing a little crush on her.

But you would be very mistaken.

Mr. Nice may have been a persona, but I am who I am. A vampire. We are not known for our soft hearts. We play hardball. We play dirty. And I have no interest in giving up my survival for a few months with a human woman. That isn't to say I do not find Brandi attractive, but I can say the same for Liza. I can say the same of a lot of women. Women are beautiful.

I dress in my favorite leather pants, a dark blue button-down shirt, and boots. I am to meet Liza downtown, where we will "hang out." A restaurant, I suppose, because she said food was involved. I do not care where we go as long as I am able to begin pushing the idea that her best option is to stay a vampire and turn me.

She is looking for Mr. Right. And here I come.

I park near the address, a large gray building in a run-down neighborhood. I wonder if this restaurant is one of these pop-ups I have heard so much about.

I check my hair one last time and snarl. *Another gray hair?* A reminder that the clock is ticking for my body.

I exit the car and walk inside the place. The smell of chicken and bread fill my nose. People are lined up, receiving plates of food. *A soup kitchen?*

I spot Liza coming from the kitchen, holding a big metal pot, which she sets on the table next to the servers. Her blue eyes zero right in on me.

Ah, she caught my scent. Tonight I am wearing a vampire favorite, Dragon's Blood cologne. The earthy cedar undertones remind the older vampires of the "good old days" when they slept in coffins or deep inside dark caves—all before the Great War, about four hundred years ago. The war pitted the old world versus those who wanted vampires to live in a more "civilized manner," side by side with humans. The latter won, of course, and since then the open hunting of humans has become illegal. Vampires still do it, but the world of law and order left the older generation feeling nostalgic for a time when vampires ruled unapologetically.

As for me, I am a creature of comforts. I do not care which side rules as long as I am left to my vices.

All right. Fine. I do enjoy modern conveniences. Air conditioning, automobiles, and credit cards are wonderful. Being hot, traveling by mule, and lugging around bags of coins is downright dismal. For a bibliophile such as myself, this whole ebook movement is phenomenal, too. At this very moment, I have millions of books in my pocket. I don't have time to read them, but they are there.

"Racker! Come on over." Liza waves at me. She is wearing baggy overalls and has her hair in two braids. She looks positively gorgeous.

I smile and go around the long line of humans. "Good evening."

Her eyes wash up and down my body. From the smile on her face, I take it that she likes what she sees. Strong arms, a broad chest, muscular thighs. *That's right, woman, underneath it all is a set of abs that can cut diamonds and a manhood capable of giving you a concussion.*

"Grab an apron," she says cheerily. "You can help bus tables and refill the drink stations."

She expects me, the once great and powerful Nicephorus, to wait on humans?

"I would love to," I say with a fake smile and grab an apron from the hook on the wall behind her.

"Tubs for dirty dishes are over there." She points to a large stack in the corner. "Just pick up anything left on the tables and then wipe down the spot if it needs it. Oh, and if you'd make sure we're not out of milk? We've had more children tonight than expected. After that, just make sure there's still plenty of hot coffee and water." She points to two large plastic rectangles with spigots.

"My pleasure."

She arches a brow. "Are you sure? You look a little…I dunno, shocked maybe?"

Game time. "Yes. I am. But entirely in a good way," I lie. "I had no idea you were such a charitable *creature.*" She knows I mean *vampire.*

She shrugs. "What else is there to do when you have nothing but free time?"

I dog-ear that comment. She has just provided the perfect argument for her remaining immortal: She sees giving time to others as her gift to the world. I could also probably get through to her by arguing how the world does not need more humans. Aren't there enough lives occupying this planet already?

When I was born in the 1700s, people had space to breathe and live and plant fragrant herbs for their homemade potpourri or raise adorable tiny animals such as miniature goats. Not that I ever wished to do that. *Much.*

"I couldn't agree more," I say. "Free time is a gift meant to be shared, not squandered."

She beams at me. "Thank you. You really surprised me just now."

That didn't sound good. It implies that I came off as uncharitable before.

As a reminder to her, I press my hand over my bat tattoo hidden under my shirt. "A side effect of living in survival mode for so long, I'm afraid. Now I can't stop giving back."

Her eyes soften as she blinks at me. "You're a sweet man, Racker."

In bed, yes. You must also add dirty to the list. Indiscriminate, too. I enjoy just about every form of sexual pleasure. Nothing is taboo as long as both parties are in raptures.

"And you, Liza, are the most interesting woman I've ever met." See, right there, I said *interesting*. If you tell a woman she is beautiful before you truly know her, she merely thinks you're giving her lip service. Ah, but comment on her uniqueness or intellect and she feels special. *Interesting* is one of those words she can interpret any way she likes—educated, driven, perplexing, kinky. The word *interesting* could mean all those. It is up to her to decide.

She blushes and goes back to work, while I try to hide my disdain for cleaning up after humans. I care not if they are destitute or homeless; it is simply wrong for a vampire of my standing to play maid to anyone. But at the moment, I must do what it takes to gain her affection. *I am Mr. Right. And Mr. Right wants forever with you, Liza. Turn me.*

I simply hope I can pull this off. Liza is unlike any vampire I have ever met, and I am unsure if my bag of seduction tricks will work. I have a feeling I am about to find out.

CHAPTER TWELVE

"Wow, you really were helpful tonight, Racker." Liza sips on a bag of O-negative while I lean back in the red kiddie chair. This section of the library is Miriam's pride and joy—a space for little humans to discover their love of reading, listen to story time, or play with colorful blocks while their mothers are off in the self-help section, wondering why they no longer feel like the sexual vixens they once were or why their asses have grown. I could tell them why— *Because getting old sucks! And immortality is the only cure*—but their asses are no concern of mine.

"And you were really spectacular, Liza. I have never known a vampire with such a kind heart, but I sensed something was different about you right away."

She looks down, batting her golden eyelashes. "Thank you."

"No, thank *you*. So tell me how you came to be like this?"

"Like what?"

"So unvampire. Because trust me, I've met plenty. They are all so cold," I lie. Well, maybe it's not a lie.

"I guess…I just made up my mind not to let being a vampire stop me from being me. I suppose you could say I saw it as an opportunity to be super-me."

"Interesting." This time I really mean it. "You never wanted power or to have your own group of human slaves to rub your feet every night?" I know I did. A foot-rub harem was the first thing I acquired after being turned and leaving Narcissismo.

And in case you're wondering, I never tattooed my slaves. A vampire only does that when they wish to keep the human around for a while. It's sort of a calling card to other vampires that says, "This human is taken." It is a practice that is considered "old school" and very rare these days.

"A slave?" Liza laughs. "Never crossed my mind. All I wanted was more of everything that already made me happy. More helping, more kindness, more self-exploration and enlightenment."

"Who *are* you?"

She giggles. "What do you mean?"

"What do you mean, *what do I mean*?"

"You are the Mother Teresa of vampires."

"God no. I'm not that selfless. And trust me, I have plenty of flaws. I'm far from being saintlike."

"Flaws? Do tell."

"Well, for starters, I hate the idea of vampire societies and the pressure to conform. I feel like some vampires are constantly judging me because I don't want to live like they do. Maybe that's why I went off on my own. I hate being told I couldn't be myself—"

"Me too. What I mean is that I think we should follow our destinies. The vampire councils, society leadership, and king have no right to interfere. If I were king, I would rule in a completely different manner—let the territories and societies determine their own coven laws based on a set of basic common laws. Today, everyone is expected to follow the same rules regardless of if they make sense, which completely discounts how unique each of the twelve territories are. A vampire in India is nothing like a vampire in, say, Peru. Some covens are newer, and some live closer to the ancient ways. Some do not want foreign vampires to enter their territories, while others enjoy outsiders and free trade." For certain though, my vision of world domination does include allowing me to do anything I like. There have to be some perks as king.

"How do you know so much about vampire law?" she asks.

I suddenly realize my blunder. Her talk of vampire self-determination has gotten me excited. I told her I have always been human, so there is no reason for me to be in the know. I need to cover my tracks.

"I have something to tell you, Liza."

"Uh-oh. This sounds like it's going to be a long conversation. Give me a minute?"

I dip my head. "Absolutely."

"Be right back."

She gets up and disappears in the back, where there's Miriam's office, a break room, and some storage closets. I know the layout of this library like the back of my hand, the result of spending endless hours here as a toddler—until people started noticing Miriam's rapidly aging son.

I start pacing around the library, fine-tuning my story. *How do I know so much about vampire laws?* I do not want to lie. And no! It has nothing to do with Brandi's lecture about hijacking someone else's happiness. But I must have an explanation. A good one.

"Okay. All set." Liza has another bag of blood in her hand. "Sorry about that, but you smell incredibly delicious. I don't want to be tempted to nibble."

She can tell I am spicy? Only bad humans are spicy. Now I have two things to cover up.

"Thank you," I say. "I appreciate you not biting me. The thing is, Liza, my time as a vampire's slave made me very unhappy. I wanted revenge, to kill every vampire I met after that." That part is actually true.

I would also add that it made me quite mad. Certifiably insane. Sometimes I would try to run from Narcissismo, and he would punish me in very creative ways—locked me in a wooden crate filled with itchy plants, beat me until I stopped crying out—i.e., until I was too in shock to feel my skin any longer—and other times he would do nothing, say nothing, which was far worse. The stress of not knowing what my punishment would be was the ultimate psychological torture. It allowed my imagination to run wild. Would he drink me to near death? Would he flog me or tie me to the back of his carriage and make me run until my legs gave out? His sadistic ways broke me.

It is no wonder I cannot trust anyone. My existence became about survival and avoiding ever being anyone's torture-pet again. *Power is the only assurance.*

"Really?" she says. "You don't seem like a vampire hater."

"I know. It's shocking, but that's probably why I smell so good to you. I am no saint either."

"It's understandable after what you went through."

"Yes, but recently I have gained much clarity. I began realizing that hating vampires isn't the answer."

"No?" She takes a long sip from the corner of the bag.

"I want to be like you, Liza. I want to become a vampire so I can do good." I swallow hard for effect to make it appear like this conclusion of mine is not easy to grapple with. "No one should go through what I did, but the only way to really change things is from the inside. Vampires can't just take a person simply because it pleases them. Humans are more than toys or food. We are family, friends, brothers, and sisters. So if I have to become a vampire to be an advocate for human rights, then so be it."

"Wow, Racker. That's, uh…" She rubs her forehead. "That's really bold."

"I know, but who better to shine a light on this issue than someone who knows both worlds?"

"You never told me who your owner was."

"Narcissismo. He's dead," I lie, "but I really don't like speaking about him. I'm sure you understand."

She bites her lower lip, flashing a bit of fang.

"What?" I prod.

"I think what you're doing is honorable, but I doubt some vampires will ever change. They're stuck in their ways—almost like their empathy died with their human selves."

"Perhaps, but the exceptions to the rules, like you, give me hope. Change is possible." *Odd.* I'm actually beginning to believe my own lie. Perhaps because I am not making everything up. My suffering was real. My motives for power are real. My general disdain of other vampires is real.

"So who is going to do the deed and turn you?" she asks.

I stare at her with directness.

"Me?" Her blue eyes go wide.

"Why not? You are kind, and I know I could trust you to do it right." If I am tasty, there is a risk that the vampire would be tempted to drink me to death before ever giving me their blood—a necessity for transformation. Also, the vampire must be ancient and powerful. Liza checks all the boxes.

"I'm sorry, Racker, but I hardly know you. We've only just become friends, and changing someone is not on my list of priorities right now."

How the hell did I land in the friend zone? Me? I know she finds me attractive, so it must be the fact that I do not share her dreams of staying human and having babies. Nonetheless, she thinks our dinner the other night was merely a friendly meal. Which means tonight really is simply "hanging out."

I think fast. Perhaps the friend zone is not a bad place to be. I can use this to my advantage.

"But we are becoming friends," I say. "Why not get to know me while you search for your soul mate and stay open to all possibilities, like you said. You are a very remarkable woman, Liza, and you've only just begun putting yourself out there. I bet you'll end up with more than one suitor to choose from. Vampires and humans alike. Why limit your options until you've truly found the right man, the one who appreciates everything you have to offer as a woman?" I do not come out and say that man is me, but I know by speaking these words, I am planting seeds in her mind. I *could* be him.

"I don't know…" She groans. "I suppose you're right. Finding my special someone comes first, but I really want children, too. That means I have to take the cure."

"I do not envy your situation, Liza. Having to decide between the perfect mate or babies who require constant care is difficult. Love of your existence or…no more travel, feeding every two hours, being a servant to ungrateful cretins who throw themselves on the floor at Target because you won't buy them a baby Yoda." Not that I'm speaking from experience. *Eh-hem.* "But only you know what is right for you."

"True. I just…I guess I still haven't given up hope that I can have both."

"If you do, then you will be the luckiest vampire in the world. As for me, I don't want to be greedy. If I find my soul mate, I'll be grateful. So many of my friends are still searching, and I doubt they'll ever be successful. I once met a vampire who'd been searching for four hundred years to meet a woman he could love." *That's right, Liza. Think long and hard about what you're asking for. A perfect man* and *children? You're a five-hundred-year-old vampire.* "He eventually gave up. He told me that if the universe planned for him to be with someone, it would have happened."

Liza sighs with longing. "I hear what you're saying, but I have to try. Of course, if I have to choose, then I will."

"No, no. Do not give up, Liza. I did not mean to make you doubt yourself," I lie. "I feel the same as you do when it comes to following your destiny." I pause, offering an intense look to demonstrate my sincerity. "I wanted to put my cards on the table with you—transparency is important in my way of life. Now more than ever."

"How so?" she asks, taking the bait. It is time to change tactics. Make her see I am not desperate or going to throw myself at her. If she wants me, she will have to win *me* from the friend zone. Vampires love the chase.

"I have been struggling with telling my girlfriend about my plans. She was once a vampire slave, too, and hates them more than anyone I know. Every time I mention I want to become one, she explodes. I don't want to lose her—she is very special to me—but I do not know how to overcome this hurdle in our relationship. She wants to stay human, and I need to do everything in my power to protect people like her." How's that for a martyr mission statement? "I just wish she would see what I'm trying to do, Liza. We all have our callings." Liza is all about callings. I know she will sympathize with me.

She finishes off her snack bag and sets it aside on the small table next to her. I can see her wheels cranking.

"That woman you came here with the other day, is she your girlfriend?" she asks.

"Yes. Why?"

"Nothing. Never mind." Liza pauses pensively. "So she doesn't like your idea of becoming immortal, and you feel it's the only way forward. That is quite the conundrum."

"Yes."

"Well, if it helps, I'm here for you."

"And I, for you. I can't explain it, but I feel like we were meant to be friends, Liza. It's like I've known you forever." Funny, when I say those words, I think of Brandi.

"Hey, how about we go out tomorrow night?" she says.

My plan is working! She is starting to see the path forward, and her attraction to me is obvious.

"What did you have in mind?" *Dancing? Drive-in movie? A little blood-exchange action while we Flix-n-chill?*

"I have a date with this guy I met last week—human. Why don't you bring…?"

What is happening? Why is she talking about another guy? "You mean Brandi?"

"Yeah, Brandi. We can all go on a double date. That way she can see not all vampires are evil bastards. I mean, we can't let my date know what I am, since he and I aren't there yet in our relationship, but that doesn't mean I can't help with your issue. I assume Brandi knows I'm a vampire, right?"

Hold the crazy vampire horses. She wants to go on a double date? And Liza is going out with other men? My plan of reverse seduction is not working.

I smile tightly, trying not to grit my teeth. "Yes, Brandi knows, and that sounds like an excellent idea. I'm sure she'll have her reservations, but I can persuade her. Absolutely." Wrong. Brandi would rather have her eyes plucked out with tiny cocktail forks than assist me in this ruse.

"Then it's a date. I'll text you the place."

"Thank you, Liza. I appreciate how supportive you are."

"I, for one, hope you change your mind and stay human. It would be good to have a human friend I can talk to after my transformation, but I respect your choice. We all have our paths. Me included."

I start to worry. "When exactly is your appointment to take the cure?"

"In a few days."

Oh no. That's not enough time to convince her to turn me.

"Didn't you mention needing to make preparations?" I say. "So you'll know what happened?"

"I did it last night. Oh, and now that the king has an entire team working on the rehumanization project, it's way easier. The case worker makes sure every vampire is prepared to enter the human world again. They even have classes and group therapy to deal with the loss of vampire-life memory."

Damned those Vanderhorsts! Always having to be the heroes.

On the other hand, I saw what Miriam went through. She took the cure before they'd figured out the correct dosage. Her side effects were not nearly as extreme as mine, but she ended up losing more than just her vampire memories. The cure shaved off an additional decade from her age and mind.

When she woke, she was reborn as a twenty-year-old with zero recollection of losing her parents, of meeting me or Vanderhorst, of having a daughter, or being turned. It was a shock when she finally realized she was thirty-two and a large chunk of her life was missing. Frankly, even though I was reveling in my wicked plans at the time, I worried for her. Vanderhorst had once again failed to protect her. He should have done proper research and understood the side effects of his concoction. But no. The great Michael Vanderhorst was so desperate to prove himself the hero, the vampire knight in shining armor, that he rushed ahead.

His arrogance has always been his downfall. The only thing I respect about Dad—I mean, Vanderhorst—is that he is quick to accept responsibility for his actions. Still, what sort of self-respecting vampire takes the blame for anything? He is the worst vampire ever! And of course he cannot become a human again because it is his blood they are using to create the cure. It has to come from a vampire with ancient, strong blood…

My thought trails off. *Dear God! I've got it.* Liza is technically a second generation and is approximately a hundred years older than Vanderhorst! And Vanderhorst has been waiting five long years, searching for a vampire who is stronger than he is.

Why? Great question.

When a vampire ingests the blood of a stronger vampire, the more powerful strain of the virus kills off the weaker form using the virus's own immune defenses. Normally, without any intervention, this results in a vampire such as Liza, who drank her maker. She was left stronger and faster, having "absorbed" the blood of a more powerful vampire.

The cure is essentially a dose of a stronger strain's immune system, the equivalent of white blood cells only. No actual virus. These interferons attack the weaker vampire virus, leaving behind a perfectly healthy human body. Of course, take too much of the cure and there are side effects.

In any case, Liza is the vampire they've been searching for. She can take Vanderhorst's place as the supplier of blood for the cure, and her blood will be strong enough to cure Michael, too.

I must make her see that the vampire world needs her blood. And so do I! Perhaps I can persuade her to provide a sample.

CHAPTER THIRTEEN

After saying goodbye to Liza, I head home and find Brandi stretched out on the brown leather couch, watching TV in the family room.

"You are still up," I say.

"Couldn't sleep." She stares at the screen, some fake docuseries about vampires from New Zealand. I don't get the humor. It makes us all seem so out of touch with the world. *As if.*

"Want to talk about it?"

"No."

I do not like seeing her upset. It annoys me. Also, I need to make amends. "I have a matter I wish to discuss with you, then." I lift her feet and sit, placing her legs over my lap.

"Oh?"

"Yes. I would like you to go out on a date with me."

She stares for a long, serious moment. "What about Liza and your great seduction plan?"

"Taking a new direction. And she would be joining us."

Brandi narrows her brown eyes. "You're asking me on a threesome?"

"As much as I would enjoying being sandwiched between two beautiful women, it is in fact a double date. Liza thought it would be nice for four of us to go out."

"Uh, no thanks." Brandi turns her attention back to the screen.

"Why not?"

"I'm not going out with a bunch of vampires."

"Only Liza is a vampire—her date is human."

"Still no."

"Please, Brandi? I need your help. Liza needs to trust me so—"

Brandi slides her feet to the floor and turns her entire body in my direction. I can almost see the angry puffs of steam coming from her ears. "So you can lie and use her? You're incredible."

"I know, but that is beside the point. I have found a legitimate reason for Liza to remain a vampire—it is something even she cannot argue with." I feel proud of myself, actually. Unintentionally, my evil plan has turned into something good. Liza lives for helping others. Her blood will change many vampires' lives, including Vanderhorst's, who wishes to join Miriam and become mortal again, too.

"The answer is still no. I'm not interested in participating in your games."

I do not see this as a game. I need more time to convince Liza to turn me. "Brandi, I will die if I am not made into a vampire. You know this."

"Then tell Liza the truth. If she's a good per-son—vampire—whatever—she'll want to help you."

I cannot take the risk. If Liza discovers my true nature, she will never speak to me again.

Suddenly, I feel a wiggling, uncomfortable sen-sation in my gut. *Guilt.* I can see in Brandi's eyes that she truly wants me to be honest, and for reasons I cannot explain, I do not wish to deny her. *She's probably a witch. Maybe a succubus.*

"You win," I say. "Come on the date with me tomorrow, and I will tell Liza the truth." Partially. One must keep some secrets to themselves.

"Seriously?"

I nod. "If it will make you happy, then yes."

"Okay," she says, "but I have one more condi-tion. You have to help me talk to my parents when they get here. I need a buffer."

She is nervous about telling them she was taken by a vampire. She fears they will not believe her. To be honest, I do not understand why anyone who knows this woman would doubt her. She's probably never told a lie in her life.

"I am here for you whether you go on that date or not," I say, actually meaning it. Shocking. "I've got your back. Always."

We exchange looks for a few long moments. I feel my heart warming and my pulse grow rapid. It is strange how a man can go his whole life and never care about anything other than himself. Then, one day, you come across a woman cowering in a moldy shower, and she becomes like a splinter you can't dig out. *Definitely a witch. But a good one.* I hate anything good. *Yet…not Brandi.*

"I am going to miss you," I say.

"Yeah, sure."

"I mean it."

She looks away at the TV. "I'm going to miss you, too."

"Maybe we will see each other again after this is all over?"

"Doubtful. You'll be off living your vampire life, and I'll be…surviving."

"You truly don't believe me when I say I will deal with the threat?" This makes no sense. I saved her once, and I would do it again. Brandi is turning out to be the one person I actually like in this world. Brave, honest, scrappy.

"I think you'll try."

"What does that mean?" I question.

She looks at me again, her brows shrugged and eyes intense with worry. "Some situations are impossible to resolve."

Not if you are me. Yes, I have succumbed to doubts these last few days, but I always overcome. "I will find a way for us both to succeed."

She nods at the floor, and her intense gaze turns somber.

"Are you certain nothing else is bothering you?" I ask.

"I guess…I don't want to be alone right now."

I am flattered that she wants my company and can find comfort in it. Almost makes me feel…good. "What flavor?"

"Sorry?"

"Popcorn. Which flavoring of sprinkles do you like?" I ask.

She smiles brightly, and I feel like I've just won a medal. "Got cheddar?"

"Coming right up."

I head off to the kitchen to make her snack. It dawns on me that I've never had this—someone to just "hang out" with and be myself. Maybe I should convince Brandi to stay a while in Phoenix.

No. Bad idea. I shake off the thought. I do not want to be near her once I am turned. And if I fail at my endeavor to be a vampire again, I would not wish her to stay by my side to watch me wither. In a way, I am thankful that my family—I mean, Miriam, Vanderhorst, and Stella—left, too. I want everyone to remember me the way I was. With an incredibly muscular body and youthful appearance.

What am I saying? I will triumph. I will be a vampire on the outside again.

CHAPTER FOURTEEN

The next day, I begin preparations for my own transformation. I am confident that Liza will turn me after I explain the truth. I will share the most critical parts but leave out the things she doesn't need to know. Such as, I was once a vampire who made other vampires leave puddles on the floor.

Step one: Explain how much she is needed in the vampire world. She could support the rehumanization project and allow another vampire to fulfill his dream to be human again.

Step two: Tell her I would like to be her partner in crime and help her leverage her clout, which she will have once everyone learns she is a gold mine for the cure. Together, we can push real change in the vampire world. Yes, yes, she thinks I mean to drive awareness about treating humans fairly, but really, I want one thing: *World domination!* If I have that, I can force vampires to accept my laws—the right laws!

Step three: Have her change me.

All I need is for Liza to sympathize with me, which requires her to see me with Brandi—my vampire-hating girlfriend. Brandi will scowl and sneer throughout dinner, and Liza will want to rescue me from my sad situation.

Around seven in the evening, I knock on the guest-room door to collect Brandi.

"One sec!" she calls out.

"I will wait in the foyer. The car is already out front." I have planned for everything to go perfectly tonight. Brandi will grow tired of the company of a vampire during dinner; we will fight; she will leave. Liza will want to comfort me, and tell her date to go home, giving me the opportunity to tell her the "truth." She will see my plan is the best and then want me by her side and turn me. Done.

I wait in the foyer and check myself in the mirror. Tonight I have my hair pulled back. I am wearing a fine Italian suit and a blood red tie.

"How's this look?" I hear a soft voice to my side.

Brandi is standing there in a short red dress with her cleavage on display like two creamy pastries begging for a bite. Long smooth legs are accentuated by strappy black heels that remind me of rope. *Mmmm…I'd like to tie those ankles up. Around my head.*

I swallow hard. "You look…um…very nice."

"Are you sure Miriam won't mind me borrowing her dress?"

Who cares? You were born to wear it. "I am certain she will not mind, but…" It dawns on me that I will not be the only person looking at Brandi's bountiful bosom and erection-provoking hips. "But

I advise you to wear a shawl."

"Shawl?"

"Yes, you do not want to tempt the wrong sort of attention this evening. A vampire would take one look at you and want to take you home—perhaps lick you from head to toe, feed you strawberries dipped in whipped cream, and then make sweet, sweet love to you for several hours."

Brandi cocks a beautifully arched brow. Her ruby red lips pucker. "I'm not wearing a shawl; it's a hundred degrees out tonight."

She does not take me seriously. I am trying to protect her.

"Fine," I grumble under my breath. "But don't blame me if you end up with a stomachache and seduced by a vampire."

"Noted."

We head outside, and I open the car door for her, catching a whiff of her hair—vanilla and raspberries. *Mmmm…Suave shampoo.* It's what we have in the guest bath. Brandi even makes the cheap stuff smell good. She is beginning to get on my nerves. First she holds me accountable, then she gets all sexy for our date, and now she smells good? *She is a horrid woman.*

The drive to the restaurant, some fondue place, is fairly quiet. I am thinking about all the various ways this evening might go sideways and making mental notes on how to respond. For example, Liza could see the logic in remaining a vampire, but still refuse to turn me. Liza's date could get in the way of having a private conversation with her. Brandi might flee the restaurant before making a proper display of her hatred for vampires, which could derail my plan to earn Liza's sympathies. The list of possible derailments is long.

"So why are we going to a cheese place?" Brandi asks.

"Pardon?"

"We're going to a fondue restaurant, yes? Isn't that a little strange for a vampire?"

"Oh, that." I shrug, keeping my eyes on the busy freeway. "Liza lived among yak herders for many years. She probably misses the curds."

"That's weird."

"She is a very unique woman. She believes in following one's dreams, which is why she is a prime example of living a full vampire life. She sees immortality as a gift to live life to its fullest."

Brandi is quiet for a long moment. "So she doesn't go around collecting people and torturing them?"

"Not all vampires are like Julia. Some are good." *Blech!*

"What kind of vampire were you?"

I give her question some serious thought. "Rotten to the core."

"You're being serious right now?"

"Yes. I was far worse than Julia."

"And you want to go back to that?"

I shrug.

Brandi scoffs.

"Do not judge me, woman. I did what I had to do. Surviving in the vampire world is not easy."

"You just said that Liza did it without being evil."

I supposed Brandi has a point. But Liza lived completely on her own, outside of societies. "She is the exception."

"I hope you will be too if you get your wish. I can see you have a big heart."

"I am afraid it is too late for me. I was raised without kindness or compassion. I only knew obedience and survival."

"That was then. This is now. You can change if you really want to. You can be a decent, caring man whether you live twelve more months or twelve more centuries."

I do not respond. Mostly because I do not wish to quarrel. Also, because I do not want to disappoint her by being truthful. I will never be good like her and Liza. I can only be myself. "We are here. Just remember, Liza's date does not know about vampires."

"Got it."

We park the car out front in the lot and go inside to the dimly lit restaurant. Liza and a thin man, hardly any meat on his bones, are seated at a booth, sipping cocktails.

Liza smiles and waves Brandi and me over to

make introductions. Liza's date is named Craig. He is wearing a tie-dyed T-shirt and has long stringy hair.

Couldn't bother with a brush for your date? Slacker!

Liza is dressed in a flowery peasant blouse and has her blonde hair in pigtails. I like her unique style. It says she doesn't care what anyone thinks, but that she's also fun.

Brandi sits down and immediately starts chatting it up with Liza. "So, Racker tells me you were a yak herder?"

"Well, not exactly. I lived with a family and helped out. You know—milking, making cheese, weaving colorful yak blankets for winter."

"That is so interesting." Brandi goes on with her long string of questions while I look on, trying not to fume.

Brandi is supposed to be uncomfortable and annoyed over sharing a meal with a vampire. This is not going well!

When Liza mentions that she spent time in Machu Picchu, deciphering hieroglyphics, I know I'm done for. Brandi is completely enamored of Liza. Meanwhile, Craig helps himself to huge gooey globs of oily melted Gruyere and Swiss while I try not to implode.

Calm. Be calm. If I am unable to earn a sympathy card this evening, all is not lost. Perhaps Liza will still see value in our friendship after I tell her the news: She is needed! And I should be a vampire again so I can assist her.

"I'm so sorry. We haven't let you gents get a word in," Liza says to Craig and me. "How's the food?"

"Runderful." Craig bobs his head with a mouthful of goop.

Brandi takes a nibble and so does Liza.

"You know," says Liza, "the flavor of this cheese reminds me of my time in Italy, working for a baker. He made the most wonderful cheese bread."

"I love baking!" Brandi exclaims.

"Oh, me too," says Liza. "Just this morning I made a jalapeño-cheddar bread that was to die for."

"I need the recipe!" Brandi says.

Seriously? Seriously, Liza. Now we are going to talk about baking? What's next? Knitting? Kayaking? Naked Roller Derby? Actually, naked Roller Derby is quite enjoyable. *God, I miss the eighties.*

"Are you all right, Racker?" Brandi asks.

"Glorious."

"Then what do you think?" Liza asks.

"About what?" I say.

"Liza just invited us to a party." Brandi's eyes are lit with excitement, so of course that means I can't say no.

"I can't go," says Craig. "I have a five a.m. hot yoga class."

"Oh, that's too bad," says Liza, who then turns

her attention to me. "How about you, Racker? You game for a little fiesta?"

This will present an opportunity to get Liza alone and talk to her. Especially because Craig is not coming. "That sounds fun."

"Then it's settled," says Liza.

We finish the meal, and Liza walks Craig to his car to say her goodbyes. She tells us she'll pull around so we can follow her.

"What's wrong?" Brandi says as we get into my SUV.

"Nothing."

"Then why do you look like a bee flew up your nose?"

"I am fine." I put on my seatbelt and try not to ruin the mood. Tonight could be my last chance to persuade Liza. The day after tomorrow is her appointment for the cure.

"I thought you wanted me to go on this date so you could make a good impression on Liza."

"Yes."

"So then?" she asks.

"Nothing."

"Well, I think Liza's awesome. Incredible, really. I'm almost glad her date is leaving so we can talk more openly. Listening to how positive and adventurous she is makes me see I don't have to be so afraid."

"Of?"

Brandi shrugs. "Vampires. After being kidnapped and tortured by one, the thought of this world being filled with Julias was terrifying. But now…" Her voice fades.

"Now what?" I snap.

"She helped put things in perspective. This world is filled with bad people, too, but I never let that stop me from living. Why should I see vampires any different?"

Uh, because a vast majority are bloodthirsty fiends and one of them has put a target on your nipple—I mean back? "That is absolutely correct, Brandi. Nothing to be scared of. After all, what are vampires but people with immortality?" *And superhuman strength and speed with a bottomless hunger.*

"I'm really glad you brought me tonight. Thank you. This is just what I needed." Brandi slides her hand on my thigh.

I won't lie, it feels good. A little too good. I slide her hand away.

"Oh, I'm so sorry." Her cheeks flush red.

I've made her feel bad, which displeases me. Especially because I am trying to do the right thing for once. I respect Brandi and do not wish to mislead her in any way. "Do not be sorry. It is just that, well, these are new pants, and you have cheese oil on your hands."

"I washed them after I ate. And you don't need to make up lame excuses. I prefer honesty. I-I get that you're…not…that you don't like—never mind."

"Brandi, I find you very attractive. Make no mistake. However, you loathe vampires, and I must become one to survive. That creates two significant obstacles. One, you're not in a position to turn me; and two, you will fear me the moment I return to my immortal state."

She gazes ahead through the windshield. "Yeah, maybe you're right."

"I know I am." I pause for a long moment. "You should stay away from me after I turn. Eventually, I betray everyone."

"Why?" she asks, an edge to her voice.

"I do not know any other way. A leopard cannot change its spots."

"You're an idiot," she says firmly.

"A human response. If you don't understand something, you dismiss it."

"See. That's what's wrong with you. You're a speciesist. You see everything as either human or vampire, when really you could be like Liza and define yourself. You can be whoever you want, Racker."

"What would you know, Brandi? You have lived less than a tenth of my years. I have survived the death of my parents, being enslaved, abused, and turned. I have lived through wars you've never heard of, and I've killed vampires a hundred times stronger to save people I care about." I took down Michael Vanderhorst's maker to save Miriam. Had I been a weak, touchy-feely pussy of a vampire, I would not have succeeded.

"Is that why you saved me? Do you care?"

"Well-that-that is not the point. I only meant…" I exhale. "I merely wanted to say that my callousness, even if it is appalling to some, specifically *you*, means that I am in a position to protect others when the 'heroes' will not because they won't tarnish their good name.

"Me? I do not care. I will gut, maim, dismember, or filet anyone if it means protecting what I value."

"So you value me," Brandi says like an accusation.

I don't see the point she is attempting to get at. Yet, I realize that she's cornered me. I cannot lie to her. "Yes, fine, I value you. Are you content now?"

She smiles smugly. "I value you, too."

I am about to ask her why she's pushing this topic when I spot Liza pulling up in front of us in a vintage red Porsche. It is a beauty. "Let's go. And no more talking tonight. Not a peep. You are putting me in a bad mood."

"What if someone at the party says hi or asks me to dance?" she says with a spiteful tinge to her voice. "Would I be allowed to peep then? Or should I find a pen and paper for silent peeping? Or maybe you'll peep for me?"

I snarl at her. "If I were a vampire right now, I would punish that insolent mouth of yours."

"Such a big talker," she throws back, not at all

fazed by my growing irritation.

"You-I—I swear, woman, you are begging for it."

"You wish." Brandi points. "She's leaving now. You'd better follow."

CHAPTER FIFTEEN

We arrive at the golf resort perched high in the hills overlooking the Phoenix valley. Several cars are in front of us, being directed to parking spaces alongside what appears to be a banquet hall. The building has large windows on almost every side, allowing us a view of the party inside. People, people, more people. From our vantage point there's a view of the sprawling city below—a blanket of lights stretching as far as the eye can see.

"Wow," says Brandi, "this looks fancy."

I agree. The people inside the venue are dressed to the nines in tuxes and gowns. "Good thing we dressed up tonight."

We park and exit the car. Liza walks over to meet us and has removed her peasant blouse. She is wearing a snug black dress that reaches mid-thigh. She must've had that on underneath.

"You look stunning, Liza," I say. Funny though, I have no urges to cover her in a shawl. Or parka, picnic blanket, or trash bag.

I glance over at Brandi's swelling cleavage and cringe. *So. Much. Bosom…* She really should put them away. What will the other males think of her?

She is not a sex kitten. She is the marrying type. I should know because I am a sex kitten. And by kitten, I mean lion. Or maybe I'm more of a saber-toothed tiger?

Screw it. I'm a pervert, a fucking animal in the sack. There is no creature in existence that represents my virility, and Brandi's breasts are distracting me!

Liza blushes, looking down at her dress. "Thank you. I don't normally get all gussied up, but tonight is special."

"What sort of event is this?" Brandi asks.

"It's an awards thing for a charity I recently started working for. Really nice people. They already had the ceremony, though, so this is just the after-party."

"Sounds fun!" Brandi claps.

"Yay…" I grumble under my breath. I am three hundred years old. After-parties are like tame brunches for vampires. I wonder why Liza would even bring us here. Then again, she has been off the grid for five hundred years. She's probably starving for social situations.

We take the sidewalk and enter the building. We're immediately greeted by two lovely women in tuxedos handing out champagne.

I thank them and go inside, instantly cocooned by flashing lights, the low pulsing beat of the music, and a vibe I cannot quite put my thumb on. Everyone's dancing and laughing. People are drinking. But there's a darkness here.

"What sort of charity did you say this is?" I yell, speaking over the volume.

Liza smiles. "VFC."

"I've never heard of it," I say.

"Vampires for Caring," Liza says proudly.

Oh no. *How did I miss it? A room full of immortals!* My stomach drops into my red socks. My secret is about to be revealed. I am Mr. Nice. Not a nice guy, like Liza believes.

I look around the room. I do not recognize anyone. Not that Mr. Nice would have mingled with the do-gooder crowd.

Liza continues, "Don't worry, Brandi. This room is filled with nothing but good vampires."

"Really?" Brandi's brown eyes light up.

"No one here looks like a vampire. Why would that be?" I ask.

Liza shrugs. "You're human. You're not supposed to notice they're different."

"But I noticed you were," I retort.

"Ah!" She holds up her index finger. "That's because I'm horrible when it comes to acting human. I've hardly spent any time with other vampires in over five hundred years. No way for me to learn."

I have lost my vampire-spotting mojo? This is not good. So is the fact that while I may not recognize anyone here, there is a strong possibility they might recognize me. I was and still am quite famous.

I need to get out of here. Fast. But I do not want to alarm Liza. *Think, think, think. What is a good excuse to leave?*

"Liza, I appreciate the invitation," I say directly into her ear. "However, Brandi's cleavage is uncomfortable around vampires, and I think it's best to leave."

Liza's blonde brows shrug with confusion. "I wouldn't have invited you if it were unsafe. Everyone here has taken a no-kill vow. Bagged blood only. And most who belong to the club are doctors, nurses, aid workers from all around the world. They're all about saving lives, not taking them."

"This is great," Brandi yells. "Who could've imagined?"

Crap. She is not helping. I have to leave! On the other hand, no one has taken notice of me yet. And I do look quite different. Before I was overly thin and slightly sickly looking. Still handsome, of course. But I had not been in good health when Narcissismo turned me. Now, I look like I could be my svelte older brother. Tan, muscular, and much sexier. "I suppose I could stay for a little while."

"Stay as long as you like," says Liza. "Oh, there's Mandy, the president. I need to say hi. Be right back."

She leaves me standing at the back of the room next to Brandi, who looks completely at ease surrounded by hungry predators. On the other hand, it pleases me to see her overcoming her fear.

No, it will do nothing to stop Julia, but I have already vowed to take care of that.

"You look agitated," Brandi says. "What's up?"

I notice a few vampire males checking her out. "I would be happier if you wore my jacket."

"You're serious."

"We are in a den full of wolves. I don't care what vows they'd taken. Vampires are vampires."

She rolls her eyes. "Fine. If it'll keep you from snarling at everyone." She holds out her hand.

I remove my jacket and give it to her. She slides it on and rolls up the long sleeves. The hem nearly reaches her knees. "Better?"

Not really. Now all I see is her cleavage in the opening of the blazer. "Let me go find a trash bag. You can wear it as a scarf."

"Stop it. Let's dance," Brandi says.

"Dance?" Well, I do love to have fun. Mr. Nice was always up for a party and wild time. That was genuine.

I offer my elbow, and we go up closer to the DJ in the front. Brandi is quite the mover. Hips, arms, lots of sexiness happening. I may have to cover her in dung to keep the men away. If only I knew where the nearest cow pasture was.

I move closer to her so the hungry probing eyes in the room see she is with me. She continues moving her hips in a fast, but sensual rhythm. Suddenly I feel like a cobra, charmed by the music of her body. I am mesmerized by her slender neck and long legs. I am enchanted by her big soulful brown eyes and pouty little lips.

Some techno-Latin tune comes on, and Brandi moves closer, nearly pressing her body to mine.

I am about to warn her off—don't want to impale the little woman—but she takes my hands and steps back, teasing me with her body. Close, then back again. Closer, then back again.

She is a dance witch. And I am under her spell. I start matching her movements, and it is like our two bodies were meant to move as one.

I am about to spin her, and she steps the wrong way. Our bodies collide, and she falls back. I stumble and land on top of her. Right on top.

Ouff!

I know everyone's staring, but I'm caught up in the sensation of her soft frame beneath me. We lock eyes.

I am not going to kiss her, but those red lips do look lonely. And what sort of self-declared fiend would I be if I did not take advantage of them?

All right, maybe one kiss.

"Um, you can get off me now, Racker," Brandi grunts out her words.

"My apologies." I roll off and get to my feet before offering my hand to help her up. "I'm very sorry."

Her face is bright red, and everyone is still staring.

I turn to the crowd. "Can you blame me for

tripping her? How else can a guy like me have a shot at a woman like that?"

Everyone laughs and goes on with their fun.

Liza appears. "Are you two okay? I saw everyone looking and—"

"My clumsy human feet." I shrug.

"I'm fine," says Brandi, "but I think I'll go find the ladies' room and freshen up."

I flash an apologetic smile as she disappears toward the restrooms.

"Shouldn't you go with her?" I say to Liza.

"She'll be fine. This is a peaceful crowd."

I frown.

"Dance?" says Liza.

I am about to decline and go wait for Brandi, but it occurs to me that this is the chance I've been hoping for. "Actually, would you mind stepping outside for a moment? I have something important to talk to you about. It's private."

"Oh. Okay. Sure."

We head toward the side exit onto a small patio area. Vampires do not smoke, so it is completely empty.

The French doors close behind us. "Liza, I wanted to say how much I appreciate the effort you've made tonight to help Brandi."

"My pleasure. I like helping others—it's my thing."

"I am glad you mentioned that because I have some news. Important news."

"Okay…?" Liza's gaze grows tense.

"A vampire friend of mine has informed me that they are in need of an ancient powerful vampire."

"For what? And who's they?"

"The vampires who are producing the cure. Rumor has it that the donor supplying the blood for the serum wants to be human again. But he can't. It means someone would have to take his place. Also, for the cure to work on him, it would require the blood of a much stronger vampire. Otherwise, it won't work."

"How did you hear about all this?" Liza narrows her blue eyes.

"Like I said, through a vampire friend. I've been doing my homework, you know, because I want to become one. I figured it might be wise to ask a few questions about this cure—just in case I change my mind later on."

Liza makes circles with her hand, motioning for me to get on with it. "And you're tell me all this because…?"

"Because that vampire is you, Liza. You're probably the only one in existence who could help the vampire who has been selflessly donating his blood for over five years."

"You mean the king. The king needs my help." Liza's lips go flat. I can tell she does not appreciate the wrench I've just thrown her way. I instantly start feeling as though this whole quest is a grand mistake.

But why do I feel bad? I am simply doing what I always do. Surviving.

"Liza, I am sorry. I should not have said anything."

"No." She reaches out and squeezes my arm. "I appreciate that you told me. I would've been peeved if you hadn't. I prefer to have the choice, yanno?"

"Yes, but…I know you do not wish to remain a vampire."

"Look. It's okay. I'm just…I was…crap!"

"What? What is it?" I ask.

She tilts her head toward the night sky. "I can't believe this. It didn't even cross my mind!"

"What?"

"The cure won't work on me. I'm older than the king. My bloodline is purer too." Her eyes tear.

Dear gods. She is right. Even if she wanted to take the cure and become human again, it won't work on her.

Wow, I am getting my way, and I didn't even have to lie and cheat for it? For once I feel like luck is on my side. Until I look over at Liza, who begins bawling. Her dreams have just been crushed. By me. Well, not by me, but I delivered the news.

I pull her into my chest and hug her. "I am sorry, Liza. I wish—I wish I had not told you." Because she would have found out eventually, and I wouldn't have been the one to break her heart.

"It's fate. Fate has spoken. I'm going to stay this way forever." She continues wailing into my shirt.

"You do not know that." I run my hand over her back.

"I should have listened to you, Racker. You were trying to tell me all this before, but I didn't want to listen. I got my head all stuck in the clouds, filled with dreams like always." She pulls back, sniffling. "Thank you for bringing me back down to earth. You're a great friend. And I will grant your request."

"What request?"

"For me to turn you."

"Huh?"

"I think you will make an excellent vampire— we need more like you, vampires who care about others, who are willing to put themselves out there and tell the truth."

Now my eyes are tearing. *She said yes! She said yes!* And I did not have to seduce her or anything. I grab her and hold her again. "Thank you. Thank you."

"Liza? Racker?" Brandi's soft voice comes from the direction of the doorway.

I turn my head and release Liza.

"What is…never mind." Brandi turns and heads back inside.

She thinks I have just lied to Liza—played her.

"Come back. It's not what you think." I follow Brandi inside. The music is still pumping strong, and people are having a good time. "I didn't lie, woman. I kept my word."

Brandi weaves through the crowd, moving too fast for me to catch up. "I did not seduce her!" I yell.

Several vampires turn and look at me. One in particular catches my eye. It is Dr. Kleen, the royal physician.

"Nice? What are you doing here?" Kleen says.

Thankfully, the music is loud. Only a few people hear him. Unfortunately, they all know the name.

"Nice?"

"Ohmygod. It's Nice."

"The Mr. Nice?"

"What's he doing here?"

The chatter starts to spread like wildfire, jumping from one set of vampire ears to another.

"Racker?"

I turn my head to find Liza staring up at me. "Is it true? Are you Baby Nice?"

Did she really have to call me that? "Do I look like a baby to you?"

"Answer the question," she growls.

I could lie. I could make up a story and attempt to save my ass, but I do not want to. Frankly, hiding behind deceptions all the time is getting old. I've rather enjoyed being myself these past few days. "Yes, it is true. However, I am only just a little evil now."

"I can't believe you duped me," Liza snarls. "I thought we were friends."

"You do not understand. Mr. Nice is…he is a lie. You have met the real me. Well, except for a handful of lies, but I am not the asshole I used to be."

Liza storms off.

The faces around the room turn to scowls and snarls.

"Oh…fuck off, you judgmental twats. You're all lucky I'm a human." *And nice. For real this time!* I head for the exit, hoping to catch Brandi or Liza before they take off. Instead, I see Liza's red car exiting the lot with a passenger. *Brandi.*

They are both gone.

Well, screw them. I never professed to be an angel. I never claimed to be good or kind or anything other than an evil bastard.

It is their fault for being so gullible.

CHAPTER SIXTEEN

Deciding not to rush home, I go to my car, away from all the judgmental vampires, where I can think. I am sure that Liza will offer to let Brandi stay with her for the night, so I will allow her time to gather her few personal items from the house. Tomorrow, Brandi's parents come to town and whisk her away. Regrettably, I will not be there to help break the news to her parents, but a promise is a promise. I still intend to hunt down Julia.

Excellent plan, you fool. How will I take out Julia like this? Julia is a few hundred years old. That night at her house, I could hardly hold the door closed for three seconds while I bought time for Brandi to escape.

My thoughts drift to Brandi's bravery—how she came back for me when Julia decided to chew on my neck. I admire Brandi for her actions then, and that admiration has only continued to grow.

I suppose that is why her lack of trust offends me. It is a far greater insult to be doubted by someone you respect.

Nonetheless, I have made a promise to ensure Julia does not catch up with her. If I cannot do the protecting, at the very least I must find someone who can.

I call Liza, but it goes straight to voicemail. *Time to grovel.* I owe at least that much to Brandi.

"Liza, it's Racker. I am sorry I did not tell you who I used to be, but Mr. Nice is not real. He never was. I invented him centuries ago, because I wanted power and respect.

"Now, I am unsure who I am or what will happen to me, but I do not wish Brandi to endure the consequences of my actions while I find that out." I go on to say how Julia is after Brandi, and I wanted to protect her—as payment for saving my life. "I don't care what happens to me, but I plead with you to ensure Brandi and her family are kept safe. Julia has marked her as property. You know what that means."

I end the call, hoping my message will reach Liza before she departs for Cincinnati. I would call in a favor from another vampire "friend," but everyone in my past would sooner dine on Brandi than assist. They are bad vampires. The worst. The sorts of fiends one finds in horror movies.

And I used to be one of them. But who am I now? I wish I knew because more and more every day, I feel less vampire, less evil, and more human. And I am still dying. *Blech!*

འ ་

I stop at the store and buy junk food—frozen pizza, chocolate cake, potato chips, and cookies. I know Brandi will be gone by the time I arrive, and I must now face my future. *I will face it with treats.*

I am going to age and die. I see no point in hoping for another path. Because when I do good, no one cares. When I tell the truth, no one believes me. When I make mistakes, it is simply an affirmation to others that I deserve my fate.

Perhaps I do.

When I finally get to the house, it is predictably void of life, and I wonder what keeps drawing me back here. I have hundreds of homes all around the world where I could finish out my final days, but something about this place soothes me.

I wander the long halls, the study, the empty bedrooms, realizing every inch of this house holds memories of laughter.

Funny how I cannot recall ever being as happy as I was here—no one judging me for my past, everyone treating me as a perfectly decent human being. The unconditional love.

It dawns on me that while I was busy deceiving Miriam, Vanderhorst, and Stella, I failed to see that the life I had here was real. I was living in a fantasy, and they were a real family offering a real home. They accepted me as one of their own.

True, they did not know I remembered my past, but at the end of the day, that didn't matter. Did it?

It was my deceptive behavior, my ego and need

for revenge that tainted everything. I could have just as easily let go of the past and taken the clean slate handed to me.

But could I have let go of my love for Miriam? I turn on the oven, place my pizza inside, and go to the wine fridge. I open a nice bottle of pinot, pour a generous glass, and head to the three-story library.

I take a seat on the soft leather sofa and stare up at the towering shelves stuffed with books. Each floor is open in the center, looking down on me. This room is Miriam's pride. She loves it, and so do I.

But did I truly love Miriam? Or was she simply part of my lie? Perhaps she was just a trophy Mr. Nice wanted to put up on his shelf, like one of these books.

Pondering, I take a sip of the velvety wine with hints of Gerber plum puree. *Mmmm…*

Perhaps the issue is that I lived as Mr. Nice for so long I forgot who I was: Steviuus Nicephorus Racker. The Mr. Nice fantasy became real. The ridiculous fake accent, gaudy outfits, and outrageous behavior. *I want more lace on my bed! I veel reep out chore entrails and feed them to randy chipmunks! I will only drink Nice Tea, the blood of humans whose names begin with the letter T.*

I smile and chuckle. The humorous part to all this is that so many vampires fell for it. The more absurd I behaved, the more they feared me.

But I was never truly happy. All that power, and

it wasn't enough.

The only happiness I've ever known was here, living with these despicably kind people. *And being myself with Brandi.*

I'm beginning to realize that the harder I pursue this dream of mine—*world domination!*—the more I lose. I am pissing away the minutes, and the clock is ticking.

In the morning, I will go to visit Brandi at Liza's house and attempt to make amends. Then I will attempt the same with Miriam, Vanderhorst, and Stella. It is time to accept responsibility and be a man. *Just…a man.*

CHAPTER SEVENTEEN

The next morning, I text Liza and ask to come over. She responds with a message: *Hurry. I need to talk to you, too. It's important.*

I cannot lie. I'm worried. I was not expecting her to agree to see me so easily. Her matter must be grave.

As I drive to her home, my heart is pounding. My palms are sweating. I didn't even bother to brush my hair.

No matter. From here on out, it is a new me. Or old me? *Whatever.* I will be an honorable man. Not a cheat. Not a con man. Not the selfish bastard Narcissismo turned me into. I will take back what was stolen: the real me.

I pull up to Liza's townhouse in a neighborhood not too far from the library. I push away all thoughts of pride. I am not here to save myself or my ego. I simply wish to clear the air and apologize.

I knock, and Liza opens the door in her hot pink satin pajamas. "I'm so glad you're here!"

"You are?"

"Yes." She grabs my hand and pulls me inside. "I have so much to tell you!" She hugs me tight and drags me by the hand to her living room, which is furnished with beanbag chairs. "Sit!" She shoves me into the brown one in the corner, nearly breaking my back.

I grunt and wince.

"Oops. Sorry. It's just…" She starts hopping up and down, clapping. "I'm so happy!"

"I see that. Care to share why?"

"'Member how you told me last night that I couldn't take the cure?"

I nod.

"Okay. Okay." She inhales slowly and exhales quickly. "Well, 'member how you also said the rehumanization project needed my blood? Well, it got me thinking last night—how I could help and do my part—so I called Dr. Kleen this morning, and we got to talking about some of their other projects. Did you know they're going to gather blood lineage information from all five hundred eighty-two societies?"

"No."

"Yes. They've already started, and they're doing it to create a blood tree—kind of like a family tree, but for bloodlines. Anyway, they've already completed mapping some of the older families, and they've actually traced my maker's lineage! Kleen says he wasn't nearly as pure-blooded as he claimed. Don't you get it? The cure *will* work on me. King Vanderhorst, the donor for the serum, is still stronger than me!" She claps again. "Woo-hoo."

"Well, that is certainly good news," I say drably. Everyone gets their dream. *Me? I'm shopping for gravestones later today. Yippy.*

"It is good news! And so is the other surprise. Are you ready?" Liza's smile is so big, I wonder how the entire thing fits on her face.

"No."

"On the way home last night, Brandi told me all about your situation—the rapid aging and why you were hoping to be turned again. You should have told me! Ohmygod. I'm so mad at you," she rambles, not sounding the least bit angry. "Anyway, I mentioned your name to Kleen. I wanted to know what your real prognosis was."

"How exciting," I say blandly.

"Not yet. But it's going to be. He told me your maker isn't dead. Narcissismo is alive."

"Yes, well, surprise. I knew that already. I lied to you. I'm sorry."

"I might forgive you. Someday."

"I will not hold my breath. However, I wish never to see the sadistic bastard again. So to me he is dead."

"And he's in jail." She smiles brightly. "Not just any jail. He's entombed in Cincinnati underneath the lab along with a few dozen others. The worst of the worst of the worst vampires. And Dr. Kleen has been testing all of them as part of his blood-mapping project!" Liza looks like she's about to explode with glee—rosy cheeks, high-pitched voice, ants in her pants. "Your maker was almost a pure-bred, made by a second-generation vampire! Which made you pretty powerful too."

I'm somehow unsurprised that my maker kept such information from me. He was, after all, the one who taught me to never reveal my true self. But I suppose I always knew I was stronger and faster than most.

I should have figured it out. "This is very interesting news, but I do not see why this is worth celebrating. My vampire blood is gone."

"Oh, oh, oh… I'm getting to that! Dr. Kleen says they've been working around the clock, trying to figure out why you were such an anomaly. And now that so many have taken the cure, two other vampires have popped up with similar situations— their memories are intact, and any reversal of aging they experienced after taking the cure is going away. The doctor thinks the cure isn't actually a cure. The serum only makes the virus dormant. It permanently puts it to sleep. For most vampires anyway."

I don't understand. "But I—"

"Don't you get it? The current formula doesn't work on everyone. For someone like me, it's probably effective forever. But for the more powerful vampires, like you, they are still maintaining some of the active virus. That's why you remember!"

Whoa. Whoa. Whoa. "You mean I'm still a vampire?"

"Kind of. He said the virus is extremely weak,

kind of limping along, but over time it rebuilds its strength."

"Then why am I aging?"

"You aren't! The cure is just reversing itself."

I cannot believe this. Why has no one told me? *Probably because they wanted me to suffer for a while.* "I am not dying."

"Nope." She jumps up and down, clapping.

"But they said I was. I have three gray hairs!"

"All I know is what he told me. In a year, he thinks you'll be back to your old self and a full vampire again. With your same old strength. He said he was going to call you this week, but I volunteered to deliver the good news."

Sure. I bet he was going to call. I blink and try to process my change in fortune. "I am saved."

"Yes."

"Will I keep my new body?" I hope so.

"I don't know."

I am unsure if I should be happy or disappointed. I put a lot of effort into this body. On the other hand, I am going to be back to my old self! Also, my blood is nearly as powerful as Vanderhorst's. I should have known.

"And now I have to ask a favor." Liza kneels in front of me. "I am begging you to turn over a new leaf. Brandi and I were talking, and we both agree. We saw so much goodness in you, and after everything I heard about this Mr. Nice—"

"Mr. Nice was a mask. But that doesn't change

what I did and why I did it. Every atrocious act was a matter of survival. Vampires feed off the weakness of others. They are predators."

"Not all of us."

"One needs allies in our world to survive. You think your friends from last night would welcome me, Mr. Nice, into their holy circle of do-goodiness?" I scoff. "Not likely." I will have no choice but to politically align with evil vampires like before.

"If you try, they might. You just need to show them who you really are."

Perhaps she is unaware of the extent of my crimes. I schemed and lied. I dusted vampires who threatened my status, and I used my power to make others spy for me or do my evil bidding. "Vampires have long memories. There are some who always will hold a grudge."

"What do you care?" she says. "Let them grudge. As long as a few good people have your back, that's all you need. And you have me." She stands and offers me her hand.

I stand, too, knowing I am at a crossroads. Soon I will be back to my old self, the most feared vampire ever to walk the earth. I could use that fear and power to continue my journey and overthrow the king. I would be right back where I was, able to spin my lies and stories to make other vampires cower.

It will be like these past five years never happened.

But is that what I truly want?

"I need to talk to Brandi." She has been my voice of reason lately. I would like to hear her opinion. Also, I still need to clear the air with her over last night.

"Brandi?"

"Yes. Where is she?" I ask, looking around the room.

"We talked for a little while, and then I dropped her off at your place last night."

"But she wasn't there when I came home." And I couldn't have arrived long after them. I only stopped at the store to fondle a few Brandi-shaped breast pastries before deciding on cookies, pizza, and chocolate cake.

"Racker, I dropped her off right in front."

"In front of what?" I ask, a bad feeling growing in my gut.

"The gate. There was a car there, too. She said it was her parents waiting for her."

I sigh with relief. So her parents took her. This is good news. "Do you mind calling her, just to be sure she is all right? I don't think she'll pick up if I call."

"Sure." Liza goes to her kitchen and returns with her cell. She punches in some numbers and hits the speaker while it rings.

"Hello?"

"Hey, Brandi. It's Liza. Just wanted to see how you're doing?"

"Super great. I had so much fun last night."

Liza's eyes fill with worry. So do mine. Brandi did not have fun last night. She was devastated by my behavior.

"Cool," Liza says into the phone. "I had fun, too. When are you coming back in town so we can party again?"

"Oh, uh, who knows? Classes start in a month, and I'm gonna be swamped."

"Really? Too bad. Well, when you get your next break, you have to come back. We need to hit that killer bar again for another drinking fest."

"Totally. Hey, I need to jam. 'Kay?"

"Sure," says Liza.

"Talk soon."

The call ends, and Liza gives me a look. "There was no super cool drinking fest last night. I took her straight home after the charity ball."

"Julia has Brandi," I say. "We have to help her."

"Racker, I'm flying to Cincinnati in a few hours. My cure appointment, remember?"

"Don't you care what happens to Brandi?"

"Of course I do, but, well, I wouldn't be much help fighting another vampire. I don't do violence. The closest I ever came was wrestling a one-foot snake in the Amazon." Liza's mouth twists into a lopsided grimace. "The snake won."

So basically, Liza is useless when it comes to taking out Julia. "I can't protect her alone. I'm too weak, still human."

Liza chews her lower lip.

"What?" I ask.

"I can turn you," she says.

"Turn me?"

"Yes. I can give you my blood, snap your neck, and you'll be a full-fledged vampire again in a matter of hours. Then you can go after her."

"What about the vampire blood already in my system?" I ask, really thinking out loud more than anything.

"I don't know." Liza shrugs.

But I do. Some of the science and data has been clear since Vanderhorst began his work, work I had to hear about around the house every freaking day. The weaker vampire strain always dies. Whatever broken pieces of ancient powerful vampire blood are still inside me will die before they have a chance to recover.

I will be the prodigy of Liza. A much weaker vampire. A commoner.

My gut starts churning. The vampire world is dog-eat-dog. Only the strongest gain respect and rise to the top.

On the other hand, I faked my way for over three centuries. People believed I was more powerful than most, yet that did not make me happy. Not ultimately.

It was Miriam, Vanderhorst, and Stella. And they never cared what I was. *As long as I was good.*

"Give me your blood. And then kill me. I have a

human to rescue."

"You really do love her, don't you?" Liza grins.

"No…"

Liza gives me a look. "I thought your lying days were over?"

"Fine. I don't know if I love her, but if she dies, I won't ever find out."

"That's a better answer." Liza steps close to me and holds her wrist in front of her mouth. "Are you ready?"

Once her blood is in my veins, she must kill me to trigger the transformation. The thought of dying still disturbs me. *For Brandi. For Brandi.*

I inhale sharply. "Yes. Ready!"

She is about to bite down when the front door explodes into a hundred splinters. In the blink of an eye, the king's guards have Liza in a headlock. I am flung to the floor like a ragdoll.

"By order of King Vanderhorst," says the largest man to Liza and me, "you two are under arrest for treason."

"Treason?" Liza whimpers.

"Yes, for violating the royal decree," says the same man. "Anyone caught attempting to turn this man into a vampire will be put to death."

How did they know? *Unless…they've been spying on me.*

Vanderhorst! He's been just waiting for the opportunity to punish me. I bet he's had people tailing me since he left. *And keeping an eye on any vampires*

I've been associating with.

Liza gives me a hard look. "Run, Racker! Run! Go save Brandi."

Oh crap. Liza starts moving faster than I have seen just about any vampire move. She starts pushing the guards back. I see what she means. She is a horrible fighter. *Who pushes another vampire as a form of attack?*

Still, it is working. I take the opportunity and run.

CHAPTER EIGHTEEN

I escape the raid at Liza's, feeling just about every acceptable male emotion under the sun. Rage, anger, wishes of a painful death toward my enemies, visions of dismembering my enemies, tattooing a photo of one of my bowel movements on my enemies' faces.

Those are all emotions, yes?

Don't care. I feel them all for whoever took Brandi. It was Julia or one of her minions. Then there are the guards who showed up and arrested Liza. Then, finally, there is Vanderhorst. I know he was behind the raid.

Wasn't good enough leaving me to wither and die alone, was it, Dad?

I stop at a mini-mart and grab some fuel—a glazed doughnut—and then decide I have no choice but to call in some favors from my army of vicious psychopathic vampires. I need help locating Brandi, and once I do, I'll need even more help to take out Julia.

My only option to prevent my army from eating me is to convince them I am still and will always be Mr. Nice. The news of Dr. Kleen's discovery is likely spreading through the vampire community, which will back my story. The risk is that they might not care and eat me anyway. It is a risk I must take to rescue Brandi.

From my car, I start making calls, starting with Vlad the Viper—he likes cars. Owns several Vipers. But I get a "Sorry. Can't help. I broke both my fangs yesterday in a horrible car accident."

Useless!

I call Mittens, the vampire unicorn. Really, she's just an old crazy woman who loves dressing as a unicorn and got turned. She was fun to party with. Very dirty fighter too. But Mittens says she's in Scotland, attending the national unicorn festival. She would never be able to get here in time.

I call Chucky the Cheeky, Simon the Sucker, Fran the Fornicator, and Murray. Just Murray. They are either out of town at the festival or do not answer.

I am ready to break my phone to pieces. How is it possible that all these bastards are on holiday at some ridiculous unicorn festival! Have they no shame? They are ruthless vampires. *Not…not…ten-year-old girls!*

I scroll through my phone, viewing name after name. The rest are in no position to confront Julia (too weak) or they have no means to track her.

I get to the last name on my contact list and stare for what seems like an eternity. He is the best tracker ever known. And he is an extraordinary fighter.

I can't. I can't do it.

But if I truly want to save Brandi, I must.

I hit call and wait for the voice to answer. "Hello?"

"Vanderhorst, it's me. Please do not hang up. I need your help."

I spend over thirty minutes telling Dad—I mean, Vanderhorst—all that I have been through since they left town last week, including meeting Brandi. To my surprise he doesn't call me a lying bastard, he does not hang up, he does not challenge me. He simply listens to every word.

And when I get to the end, there is nothing but silence.

"Vanderhorst? Hello?" *He hung up.* Why wouldn't he after everything I put him, Miriam, and Stella through?

"I am still here," he says.

"You are?"

"Clearly. But what I do not comprehend is why you are telling me all this."

"Because I need your help."

"I am the last person you should call for that."

"Let me rephrase." I clear my throat. "It is Brandi who needs your help, and think whatever you want about me. I do not care. I deserve your hate. But she is not me. She is good—just some girl who took the wrong bus and got snared in Julia's trap."

"What's it to you?" Vanderhorst asks. "In your mind all humans are expendable. Except my wife, whom you can't have."

If there's any hope of getting his assistance, I must make amends. Time to put it all out there. "I am sorry for what I did to you. And your wife and daughter. I know now what I threw away. I know why I threw it away. What I don't know is how to make things right." I go on to spill my horrid guts to the one vampire I have vowed to destroy. I tell him about Narcissismo, about how he taught me to wear a mask of deceit, and how I became lost in the lie. Mr. Nice never existed. Only my need for power made him real. "But that is what I have learned, Vanderhorst. The family you invited me into is the only real thing I have known since my parents were taken. And while I have to atone for my sins, I will not stand by and allow this lovely human and her family to be destroyed by a predator like Julia."

"How do I know you're not putting on an act now, only pretending to be sorry because you're after something? It might be another trick."

"It could be, but I know you, Vanderhorst. You would never turn your back on someone who needs you. Someone being taken advantage of by a vampire. Your conscience won't allow you to gamble with *that* life. And, frankly, your feelings about me are irrelevant in the situation."

"True, but there is still the matter of what you've done. If I help her, I want something in return."

"Name it. Anything you want."

"I spoke to Dr. Kleen right before you called. I know you're going to turn back to how you were."

"And?"

"You will go to prison until you turn into a vampire again. And once you do, entombment. For eternity. That's my price. If you think so highly of this woman, if you care for her so much, and you've truly changed, then you will make this sacrifice."

Entombment? It is punishment reserved for the evilest of vampires. *Oh. Wait. I guess that was me.* I can't imagine being stuck in a dark, cold, steel box until my body is so weak, I disintegrate. I hear some vampires never dust. They become petrified mummies. Still alive! The thought sends a chill down my spine.

On the other hand, if doing this will save Brandi and make things right with Miriam and Vanderhorst, then I have to do it. At least they will know I am telling the truth. Their time was not wasted on me. They changed my heart.

"I agree," I say. "Prison and entombment."

"I will have those guards your friend pushed around take you to Cincinnati. And no funny business, or I'll call off Brandi's rescue."

I forgot about Liza. I will have to find a way to

make things right with her too. She's been arrested. But first, I need to make sure Brandi is safely retrieved.

"How will you get Brandi back?" I ask.

"You let me worry about that, Nice."

"Racker. My name is Steviuus Nicephorus Racker. My vampire master called me Racker."

"Then why Racker? Are you still his slave?"

I inhale deeply. For once, this oaf is right. "No, I am not."

"Then?"

"Then call me Steviuus."

"Sounds like a sweetener."

That is right, Vanderhorst. Because I am Mr. Sweet now. "Call me whatever you like, just save the girl." I pause. "And one more thing, please tell Miriam I am very sorry. She was a good mother to me. If it weren't for you both, I would not be who I am today."

He doesn't respond immediately. Then, "I will pass along the message. After you've fulfilled your end of the bargain."

He wants proof I've changed, that I am honest. I silently curse him—the man who raised me, who hates me, who treats me like a human being and is there when I need him. *God, I hate myself for liking him so much.* "Thank you. And good luck, Dad."

"Likewise…son."

CHAPTER NINETEEN

The next morning, I am beat after a restless night.

I have made a deal once again to trade my life for Brandi's. *Being good is getting exhausting. How does Vanderhorst do it?*

Around ten in the morning, I arrive at the private airport where the king's guards' jet awaits to take me to my fate. I spot Liza being ushered up the staircase by two guards. My inner vampire stirs with anger. The outcome of her situation must be rectified, especially because she did not do anything wrong. Not technically. I would have become a vampire again with or without her help. I will make sure she is freed before I am locked away.

I walk up the staircase and am greeted by one of the guards dressed all in black. Most guards are not incredibly powerful, but they are well trained. They know how to work as a team to overcome vampires who are much stronger. They also carry weapons such as chocolate-coated bullets and chocolate spray.

"Good morning, sir. You may take the seat over there." He points to a seat next to Liza.

"Thank you." I go over and sit with her. She's still in her hot pink pajamas.

"So they caught you, huh?" Liza sighs.

"Not exactly. I had to—"

My cell rings. It's Miriam. "Hello?"

"Nice? I got a text from Michael just now, and it was very suspicious. He said he was in Cincinnati and would be staying a few days. And when I asked him if he was able to track down your friend, he said he had a lead, but she got away. Does that sound strange to you?"

Yes. Because one thing I know about Vanderhorst is that he has worn many hats over the years, one of them being a detective. He loves a good mystery. Like a dog with a bone. Once he gets a whiff, he won't stop.

I, too, love a good puzzle, but this does not qualify. I know exactly what is going on. Vanderhorst would not have given up so easily on finding Brandi. He would not be heading to Cincinnati and abandoning the deal he made with me. He's willing to do anything to have me entombed.

"Something is wrong," I say. "He is in trouble."

"I thought so too."

"Did he mention where he was going?" I ask.

"Vegas. He found out that the vampire who took your friend recently applied for a visa."

Societies require a vampire to request a visa before entering their territory. I always ignore the rule. I was never law abiding. Neither is Julia.

So why would Julia apply? She knows I'd come

looking for Brandi. Obtaining a visa would leave a paper trail. *An easy-to-follow paper trail. A trap.*

"Did he say anything else? Any specifics where he'd start looking?" I ask Miriam.

"No."

All right. Where would I go? Where would I start looking if I were Vanderhorst? The wheels start turning. Julia's professions are bad interior designer and madam. The latter is what she is known for among the unsavory vampire crowd.

All I need to do is start asking around. The problem is, if I get anywhere near one of those vampires, they will wish to snack on me. I still smell delicious and human.

"Not to worry, Miriam. I will find him. I will get him back."

"How?"

"I have spent my existence as an evil vampire. I know how they think and where they hide. There isn't a trick I haven't seen. I will call you with an update in a few hours."

"Thank you, Nice."

"Steviuus. I go by Steviuus now."

"That sounds like a sweetener."

"That's me. Mr. Sweet." I end the call and look at Liza. "You're going to have to turn me."

"What? Are you crazy? I'm under arrest and facing execution for almost doing it yesterday."

"Then you have nothing to lose."

"Racker, I really can't—"

"What is going on here?" says the head guard. I think his name is Wallace or Wilfred. Something with a *W*. I go with Wallace.

"Wallace, I have just received a call from—" I catch myself from giving the incorrect information. "From the king's brother's wife. Freddy Vanderhorst has been taken. We need this flight to go to Vegas."

"My name is Wilber. And nice try. I have my orders. You two are to be taken straight to Cincinnati. Also, the king hates his brother."

The king doesn't hate his brother; this is simply part of the bigger lie I discussed earlier. When Freddy took over as king and assumed Michael's identity, they needed to come up with a reason for Miriam's departure back to Phoenix and being seen with a man who looks just like the king. They told everyone that Miriam was now with Freddy, the nicer twin. The brothers pretend to be rivals over this, but they are actually quite close.

"Call the king," I say. "Tell him what I just told you. Let him decide if we should ignore the fact that Freddy is in danger."

The guard stares for a long moment. "Fine. I'll make the call."

Meanwhile, the other guards start preparing the plane for takeoff—closing the door, starting up the engine, and coordinating with the control tower.

A minute later Wilber returns. "He says he will send a group of guards to Vegas."

"But we are only an hour away."

"And," the guard continues, "we should go immediately to assist. We are much closer than his men, and he doesn't know what sort of support we will get from the Vegas Society of Night Buffet Lovers. He says everyone's in Scotland for that big unicorn festival."

Night buffet, meaning hunting down unsuspecting drunk tourists for snack time. "Okay then. Let's get moving."

Wilber tells the men and then goes to the cockpit to inform the pilot.

I take my seat next to Liza.

"Well?" she asks.

"My dad is in trouble. And if you hurry, I will be turned by the time we land." I give her a look. She must know how serious I am about this. "He is a good man, Liza. Far better than me. I cannot allow anything to happen to him."

"They're never going to give me the cure if I do this." She looks at me with pleading eyes.

"Tell them I tricked you. That I lied."

"Why would I say that?" She frowns.

"Because I am Mr. Nice. They will believe you and punish me instead." Even if I save Vanderhorst, my past won't be forgiven. "Please, Liza. I will do everything in my power to make sure you are not punished. Please?"

"Fine. Open wide." She chomps down on her finger and then shoves it in my mouth. I wrap my lips around the digit and suck.

Yuck! Blood tastes terrible! Just as I am about to make a sour face, she takes hold of my head and snaps my neck.

CHAPTER TWENTY

When I wake on the plane, I am alone, it is dark outside, and my nose feels like it is on fire. *Gah! So many smells! So many sounds.* I can see everything clearly despite the lack of light.

I pop up from my seat and start feeling my face. Then my muscled pecs and washboard abs. Everything is hard as a rock. *Dear gods. I'm back! I am a vampire again!* I am also still a very sexy man. Phew.

My moment of jubilation quickly retreats into fear. Well, not fear, really. I don't actually feel afraid. More confused. *Where did everyone go?* I head to the front of the plane and spot a note sitting on the control panel.

> *Racker: We went to rescue the king's brother. I'm helping them with tracking to cover more ground. Sorry, couldn't wait for you to wake up.—Liza*

They went without me? But how the hell do they think they'll find Julia? I'm the one with the seedy network. I'm the one with the evil mind. They have no hope of hunting her down, let alone avoiding one of her traps.

I call Liza, and it goes to voicemail. I do not have any of the guards' information, so that is not an option. I can only call Miriam and ask for Freddy's number.

"Hello?" Miriam's worried voice comes through the phone.

"I need Freddy's number."

"Why? What's going on? Where's Michael?" Her voice is pure panic.

"I am still working on it. But I need to speak with the king."

"I'll text you his contact information, but please call the minute you hear anything. I love him. I love him so much…" Her voice fades into a sob. "I can't lose him. Not after everything we've been through."

Her pain tugs on my cold heart. I see now that I do still love her, though it is nothing remotely romantic. It never was. Miriam had merely been a thing to conquer, to show the world that I could take away something from the legendary Execution-er.

"Do not worry, Mom. I mean, Miriam. I will find him. I vow it." I end the call and dial Freddy the moment his contact hits my phone.

He picks up immediately. "Yes?"

"Vanderhorst, it is I, Steviuus, formerly known as Mr. Nice. I need to know where your guards went with Liza, the woman who was on the plane with me."

"You're not with them?" he asks.

There's no time to explain. "I had the flu. They had to leave me behind, but I'm feeling better now. Where did they go?"

"You had the flu a few hours ago, and now you're all better?"

"I am a very fast healer. Where did they go?" I repeat.

"Julia was last seen at some underground vampire bar called the Randy Unicorn. They think that is where my brother went."

Oh no. I knew this was a trap. But does anyone consult the evil vampire? No. They just run off playing hero. If they'd bothered to include me, they would have learned that the Randy Unicorn is where the most deranged immortals hang out. Mercenaries, human traffickers, disco junkies, and your general perverts.

My kind of evil crowd. Used to be, anyway.

Julia was likely expecting me, but if Vanderhorst showed up, they would have recognized him as Freddy or as Michael. Their faces are well known. And if he started asking questions, they would have told him they'd seen Julia in the back room, playing pool or doing shots, which is code for *"We're going to dump you in the dungeon."* Really, it is just a big pit with a trapdoor. I used to find it amusing to watch ignorant vampires or humans wander into the establishment and be told there was a party happening back there. *Then boom. Trapdoor!*

"I will start my search there. How far away are

your other men?" I ask Freddy.

"Another hour."

I cannot wait that long. "I'll keep you posted."

"Why are you doing this?" Freddy asks. "You couldn't care less about my brother."

"Why does it matter if the result is he stays alive?"

"How do I know you're not just trying to hunt him down so you can kill him yourself? We all know you'd do anything to get my sister-in-law."

See. This is what I was talking about, friends. No matter what I do, I will never be allowed to change my spots. The vampire world wants me to play this role because it makes them feel like "good vampires." They can point to me and say, *Bad. Bad!*

I do not wish to argue with Freddy, and I do not have time to convince him of my true motives. "I plan to save your brother so he will owe me a favor. And then I will force him to give me ten red horses. For my wedding. With his wife," I lie.

"I knew it."

"Yes, well, do you want me to save him or not?"

"Yes, but this isn't over. And no, you cannot have Miriam. My brother and she belong together. You belong with...with...I don't know *what* you belong with, but it isn't her."

He is right. I belong with a woman who is unincumbered by public opinion of me. I belong with someone who not only sees me for who I am, but sees my potential. I belong with...Liza!

Wait. No. That doesn't feel right. Liza is beautiful and independent. I enjoy how she teaches me new things. I appreciate her more than words can say. However, when I think of Liza, it is as a friend. I trust and respect her.

But do I want to hold an all-night lovemaking session with her? No.

Do I want to sniff her hair every day for the rest of my life? No.

Do I want to cover her in cream cheese and roll her in coconut shavings? No.

But I sure the hell would like to with Brandi. *Make a little flambé in the sheets, if you know what I mean.*

"Let us discuss this matter later," I say. "At the moment, your idiot guards have made a grave error and have likely fallen into the same trap as your brother. I must go."

CHAPTER TWENTY-ONE

I have to order a ride from one of those apps to get to the Randy Unicorn across town in a neighborhood frequented by immortals. Dangerous, sadistic immortals. Just like I used to be.

Fun fact, I once spent so much time here that Sin City was almost renamed Nice City. I would rent a huge penthouse and invite vampires from all over to come play. My parties were legendary, nothing off-limits—whips, chains, chocolate chip cookies. Years later, I would use their debauchery against them when I required a favor. *Remember how you dressed up as a squirrel and licked everyone's nuts?* The photos I took came in handy.

My ride drops me in front of the bar. It is evening, the streetlamps casting a dark purple hue over everything and—

Oh, wait. That's just my new vampire eyes. Funny, I never imagined it would feel strange being a vampire again. And a weak one at that. Yes, I can probably open a jar of pickles without a problem, but I move about as fast as a house cat. Faster than a human, but not so impressive for a vampire.

It's going to take a miracle to convince anyone I

am still Mr. Nice, a force to be reckoned with.

I knock on the rainbow-painted door of the Randy Unicorn, and after a few moments, it pops open. They inspect everyone through a camera mounted above.

"Mr. Nice, you—you've returned," says the short man with a long red beard. His name is Pike. "You look so different." He leans forward and sniffs me. "You are a vampire again!"

"*Jesss*…back and better *zan* ever!" I say in my old crazy accent.

"Well, you look, you look amazing." Pike eyes me in my jeans and T-shirt.

I know Pike swings both ways—really all ways, with anything that breathes and some things that don't—however, I have no time for kink tonight.

"Zank you, my friend!"

"Come in. Let's get you a drink." He heads through a set of double doors and enters the inner sanctum of the bar, which looks just like one would imagine for an evil vampire bar. Dimmed lighting, dark walls, dark floors, and a Ping-Pong table. There is nothing randy about this place nor sparkly and unicorn-esque.

"I could use a Nice Tea," I say, following behind Pike, noting the establishment is about halfway full. The other vampire patrons, seated around the room, give me side glances, but without my cape, red frilly lace shirt, and leather pants, I doubt they'll recognize me unless they get a good look at my face or hear my voice.

"I'm so sorry, sir," says Pike. "We only have O-negative snack bags. Or there's a guy in the closet I'm serving for cocktail hour. He's a serial killer. Extra-spicy. Twenty bucks per suck, but for you, on the house." Pike goes behind the bar.

I belly up in front of him. "Actually, *zi* Nice has *zi* favor to ask. I am here to take my vengeance on that vile *Vanderhorststs*! Have you seen him?"

Pike's eyes light up. "Oh. That sounds exciting. But no. He hasn't been here."

"No…?" I lean forward, eyeing him suspiciously.

"No." Pike steps back. "I swear."

"If choo are lying, I will reep off your eyelashes and shove them up your nose!" *Wait, that did not sound very scary or Mr. Nice-ish.* "And I will pluck off one of your testicles and feed it to your other testicle!" *There. Better.*

Pike holds up his hands. "I would never lie to you, Mr. Nice. Not after what you did to Larry the last time you came here."

Ah…Larry. He was the sort of vampire who enjoyed nibbling on people in a coma. Who does that? I mean, I have done evil things, but there has to be a line. Nibbling on the comatose is simply depraved. Anyway, Larry once swiped my drink from the counter when I had my head turned, and then lied about it. I tore off his manhood and stapled it to his forehead. Well, really I used darts from the board over there on the wall. No stapler handy at the time. I told him if he ever removed it, I would rip out his tongue and staple it where his cock used to be.

I turn my head toward the man sitting in the corner with a decade-old shriveled sausage skewered on his forehead. "Nice to see choo again, Larry!" I say cheerily.

Larry scowls and goes back to his card game with another man.

"Not very friendly," I say. "It is as if he holds a grudge." I sigh for effect. "*Veel*, if you haven't seen Vanderhorstsst, how about my old friend, zi fabulous miss Julia? I hear she might be setting up a new houzz of pleasure, and I am in zi mood for a tensome."

"Julia was here a few days ago, but she said she was just passing through. She came in looking for a place to stay for the night—her and her inventory." Pike winks.

So Julia was traveling with humans. I must follow her trail and see where it leads me. "Where did she stay?" I ask.

"What happened to your accent?"

Crap. I dropped it by accident.

I scramble for an absurd excuse that fits Mr. Nice. "This is my new accent." I wave my hands in front of my face like a magician doing an amazing trick. "I decided to change it. Right now. Here at your bar. It is a great honor for you to witness my transformation. Now where did she go?" I say flatly.

"Um, um…I think she landed at Old Man Connelly's place."

Old Man Connelly, huh? Connelly is probably one of the oldest humans to ever be turned. He was in his eighties. The man still lives on the ranch he owned a hundred years ago. How humans haven't caught on to him is beyond me.

I am about to take my leave when I hear cheering in the back room.

"Who's in the fun pit?" I ask.

"Just some human who wandered in. No one special."

"And what torture are we using today?" I ask.

"Snakes."

"I love a good snake pit." I drop my smile. "I want to see." Mostly, I don't trust Pike or any other vampire. We are not honest folk.

Pike's eyes shift away from my face. "Sorry, sir, it's a private event today. A, uh, birthday party."

He is lying to me.

I reach across the bar, pull Pike's body over the counter, throw him on the floor, and rip off his ear. I yell into the bloody piece of flesh, "Try again!"

Pike whimpers in agony, and I cannot lie; it feels marvelous to be cruel. I missed the exhilaration of making others fear me.

"Testing. One! Two! Three! Now tell the Nice who is back there, or you will be joining Larry with the penis art on your face." I reach for the zipper of Pike's pants.

"Don't hurt me, Nice."

"I will not hurt you nice. I will hurt you bad…" I say in an ominous tone.

"It's Vanderhorst. He's back there," Pike whimpers.

I knew it! But what about Liza? "Who else?"

"Just a bunch of customers. And Julia. She's auctioning off his blood."

I exhale sharply. This is not good. Vanderhorst is over four hundred years old. Any vampire who drinks his blood will instantly be stronger and faster than most. If they've been handing out Vanderhorst shots back there, it's going to make his rescue more difficult. *I'll be outfanged.*

"I'm not finished with you." I give Pike a kick in his side and toss him over my shoulder. I shove him in the closet with his serial killer appetizer, locking the door. "Anyone touches him and their ears will be next." No one in the establishment moves a muscle.

I march through the black curtains into the back room, which is basically a twenty-by-twenty room with two pool tables. The trapdoor between them is covered with a ratty Persian rug, and Vanderhorst is sitting on top of it, tied to a chair. A man in the corner has his hand on the release button.

I bet there is something very hideous and painful awaiting him down in that pit. Otherwise, he wouldn't be sitting so still.

Vanderhorst's dark eyes meet mine and go wide

with panic. He probably thinks I'm here to partake in his demise.

"Nice, what the fuck are you doing here?" Julia scowls.

Before I answer, I survey the room. There are eleven other vampires, who look like they belong to that Night Riders motorcycle gang, best known for their love of softball. They host the annual vampire championship. But do not let that fool you. These are not nice men. They're large, they're hairy, and they enjoy a good disembowelment.

My mind races for the best way to subdue this room of callous vampires. *I got nothing.* Time to wing it. "No, Julia. The proper question is what are *you* doing here? With him?" I snarl at Vanderhorst.

"What happened to your accent?"

"Nice two-point-oh does not have time for accents. Also, I am much too interesting already, and it is unfair to the other vampires. Now answer my question." I narrow my eyes.

"Well, as you might be aware, *someone* screwed up my business back in Texas. So here I am in Vegas, checking out a few possible new locations to reopen, when I get a call from Pike, asking if I'd like to help him make a few extra bucks selling off a fresh catch." She smiles. "And now you showed up! It's my lucky day." Her smile melts away. "You still owe me a house."

"And you shall have it. Whichever one you want, but Vanderhorst is mine…" I growl. "Now, everyone leave before I rip out your livers and stuff them with savory herbs." That was a terrible threat. *What is the matter with me?* "Then feed them to pigs while I snack on the rest of you, starting with your nipples." *Better.*

The men stare, but do not move, so I add, "In case you haven't noticed, I am no longer human. The cure doesn't work on powerful vampires like me. Ancient. Deadly. And filled with creative ways to dice up your male parts."

The men exchange glances and zip from the room, leaving me alone with Julia. *Ha. My old tricks still work!*

"Untie him," I say.

Julia steps in front of Vanderhorst and crosses her arms. "Why would I do that?"

"Because he and I have a score to settle."

Julia laughs. "No way. Freddy Vanderhorst is mine. Besides, you don't need to free him to settle up." She looks at Michael. "What better way to get revenge than to dust him? After we sell off his blood. Which is delicious, by the way."

Crap. Julia drank him? That means she is about a hundred times stronger than me. I am average strength and speed now, since Liza sired me. Luckily, Julia does not know that.

I must avoid a physical confrontation so she does not find out. *Or...I could...*

"That is where you are wrong, woman. This is not the king's brother. Freddy is currently sitting on the throne and has for over five years."

"What?" Her red eyebrows arch.

I nod. "Exactly. And this man is my nemesis, Michael Vanderhorst." I shake my head and walk over, circling him like a shark. "He stole the love of my life, he stole my power, and he turned me into an infant." Not entirely true. I drank too much of the cure. "Unfortunately for him, he let me live, and now I am back." I grab the top of his head and pull his neck to one side.

"What are you doing, Nice?" Vanderhorst snarls.

I am doing the only thing I can to even the playing field with Julia. I bite down and taste the coppery sweet syrup on my tongue.

"Sonof—gahh!" Vanderhorst cries out, jerking around in his chair.

I release him, feeling his blood flow through me, mingling with my own and transforming me into something far more powerful.

Now I'm back. I stare at my hand and flex my strong fist.

"You're right," says Vanderhorst. "I should have killed you. When I found you in the coat closet at headquarters, crying and hungry, I should have let you starve. Because I always knew you were a loser. A sad, deceitful joke of a vampire who acted like a fool. Miriam never loved you and never could because you're weak, you're an idiot, and no one respects you. They never have."

All lies, and he knows it. He used to nearly wet himself when I walked into a room. Still, the words coming from his mouth set off a chain reaction. Memories. Most of them from when I swore to destroy him.

I almost succeeded.

At one point, I had his woman; I framed him for treason and made him into an outlaw. He lost everything and had to live on the run, hunted by every other vampire out there. We caught him, of course. And I got within an inch of having him executed. My plan would have worked if it weren't for Miriam. She was supposed to testify against him after his apprehension. She chose to put her faith in him instead.

I snarl down at Michael Vanderhorst. The pain this man caused me, the humiliation. All because I stepped up and protected his woman when he failed. He should be thanking me, not ridiculing me.

"Do it," Julia says. "Kill him. Then we'll tell the world that his brother sits on the throne and have him removed. The people will want a new ruler, someone ruthless and cutthroat. They'll want you." Julia steps in close and grabs my arm, her green eyes intense. "You can bring back the old ways. No more of these stupid laws that treat us as children and tell us to be good little vampires. We are predators, and it is time for us to take our places at the top of the food chain once again. With you at the helm."

My entire body tingles with the most delicious drug in the world: power. Being ruler is what I've always wanted. To reshape our societies. To be above the law and do whatever I like. No one could threaten me, stop me, or make me their slave again. *King Nice.*

"Do it," Vanderhorst says. "Dust me. But it won't change who you are. You will always be worthless, unlovable, and untrustworthy. Just like I told your mother."

I raise my hand, the anger pulsing through me as savagely as the new blood in my veins. "I just want this moment to sink into your head, Vanderhorst. You are sitting here trapped, defeated, and at my mercy." I grab him, complete with chair, and zip over to the wall. I slam my hand on the button, and Julia falls into the pit.

I hear her screech as she hits the bottom, followed by a groan. "Nice! I'll kill you!"

I set Vanderhorst down in his chair. He looks up at me with those dark eyes, his face flooded with confusion.

"I do not want to hear a single sound from your mouth." I lean down, putting us almost nose to nose. "No one gets to tell me who I am. Not even you. And I have decided to be a better man." As I say the words, I feel stronger than ever. I have found what I lost, what was stolen from me three hundred years ago. I am a good man on the inside. Vampire on the outside. "I win."

CHAPTER TWENTY-TWO

I untie Vanderhorst, who remains quiet and has dark circles under his eyes. He looks a little drained. Pun intended. Julia is in the pit, which is actually filled with lamp oil. I think Pike is quite possibly the stupidest vampire to ever exist. One match and the entire building will go up in flames.

Maybe not such a bad thing.

I stand at the edge of the pit and watch her trying to scale the slick oil-coated walls while ranting, "I'll kill you, Nice! From the inside out. From top to bottom! I'll rip out your hair!"

"Someone's cranky," I mutter. "And it's Stevi-uus now. Or you may call me Mr. Sweet." It has a ring to it. "And because I am so sweet, I will consider allowing you to live," I lie, "if you tell me where Brandi and her parents are."

"Brandi?" Julia cackles into the air. "How should I know? I haven't seen her since Houston."

Hmph! She wants to play hardball, does she? I leave the room and go to the closet. I open it to find Pike cowering with his hand over his ear. The serial killer simply stares at me with wide unblinking eyes. Probably in shock.

"Oh, stop," I sneer at Pike. "You behave as if it is the first time you've had a body party removed."

"It is."

"Well, then, you've been missing out." I flash a glance over at Larry, who is all smiles. Looks like he just won a hand. Good for him. "I need matches," I say to Pike.

"Why?"

"You *know* why."

"But-but we never light the pit," he stutters. "It's only a threat."

So he is not as stupid as he looks, which is pretty stupid. One ear and all that.

"Well," I say, "I am a vampire of actions, not words. And if Julia doesn't tell me what I need to know, she's going up in flames with your grimy, smelly bar."

"But I—"

"Matches. Now," I say, lowering my voice. I always found that getting quieter is much scarier than getting louder.

"Next to the register."

I slam the door shut again. Pike starts pounding to let him out, pleading for me not to burn down his bar.

Now, why would I do that? He captured Vanderhorst and started selling off his blood. Oddly, that really ticks me off. I am the only one allowed to torture him. He's my dad. Or nemesis? Whatever. He's family. Same thing.

I go for the matches and return to the back room. Vanderhorst is slumped against the wall.

"There's a delicious snack in the closet," I say. "Why don't you refuel while I light the grill?"

Vanderhorst looks at me, then at the pit. "I think we should wait for the royal guards to arrive. She needs to be brought to justice. The right way."

I raise a brow. "I think the lack of blood in your body is warping your head."

"You claim you've turned over a new leaf," Vanderhorst says.

"You are trying to tell me that you wouldn't light that cretinous woman on fire if it meant finding Miriam?"

"I, well—"

"See. This is what I'm talking about, Vanderhorst." I shake the book of matches at him. "You overthink things instead of acting. But your need to be the upstanding hero won't protect those you love. It is action and willingness to be the ruthless cutthroat villain when called for." I point to myself. "I do not fear that. Never have. And it is why you still have a wife. I'm willing to put every-thing on the line for those I care about. Consequences be damned."

"Such inspiring words from a man who wore pink pleather pants for a few decades and declared himself the official snack of the vampire nation. Didn't you even try to trademark it?"

That was actually pretty funny. I had immortal

women lined up around the block for a taste. Of course, it helped that my lovemaking was extremely powerful.

"Say all you want about my Mr. Nice days." I raise my chin. "It won't change the fact that I stepped up and took out your maker when he was about to slaughter Miriam. Meanwhile, you stood there frozen with thoughts of consequences."

I see his eyes grow darker, his lips get flatter. "I need to eat." He leaves the back room. A few moments later I hear the sounds of a hungry vampire taking his fill of a delicious spicy meal. *Nom, nom, nom...*

"All right, Julia." I return to the edge of the pit. "Now or never. Where's Brandi?" I strike a match and hold it over the pit.

Her green eyes are wide with fear. "Nice, we're old friends. Don't you remember? Ten-for-one night? Those fun games we used to play in my bedroom—duck, duck, human?"

I won't lie. I did enjoy chasing the humans around the circle before drinking them, but that was the old me. The Nice me.

"I remember everything, including your fangs in my neck." I push my arm out further. "Last chance. Match is almost done, and I'm not about to burn my fingers."

"Okay. Okay! I'll tell you what I know, but it's not the information you're looking for."

I blow out the match and toss it behind me on

the floor. I pull off another match, ready to strike it. "I'm listening."

"Romanovich hired me to catch her. He knows I'm good at that—filling special requests."

"Why did he want her?" I ask.

"Her parents are Hugo and Katarina Botellino."

I'm not sure what that's supposed to mean.

"You mean *the* Botellinos?" Vanderhorst appears at my side, wiping up the dribbles of red blood from the corners of his mouth. The front of his suit is covered in blood. He looks very refreshed.

"Yes," Julia replies.

"Who are they?" I ask, feeling a heavy weight in my gut, like I am about to receive some very bad news.

Vanderhorst replies, "They are rumored to be Keepers who broke away from the traditional doctrine and started their own, well, for lack of a better term, anti-vampire cult."

Keepers are the term for vampire hunters, but it is more involved than that. Before the Great War three centuries ago, Vanderhorst's maker feared his side (which favored today's civilized way of living peacefully hidden among humans) might lose. In secret, he trained a multitude of families how to hunt and kill vampires. He wanted humans to stand a fighting chance should the revolution fail.

No one knows how many different families and humans he trained. Could have been hundreds or thousands. Not even the Keepers were told. He figured it was best to leave their numbers and identities a secret even from each other, in case a Keeper was ever captured.

Centuries later, after a great victory, Vanderhorst's maker would come to regret allowing humans to be in charge of this world. *Too destructive. Too addicted to instant gratification.* Vampires are all about the long term since they plan to live forever. *Quite the conservationists, I must say.*

Vanderhorst's maker attempted to spark another revolution to undo the last three centuries of vampires living in the shadows, starting with going after the Keepers. He wanted vampires to rule the world. The coup ultimately failed, but no doubt his actions left a sour taste in the Keepers' mouths. The ones who survived, anyway. The vampire who trained them turned on them.

"Are you certain Brandi's parents are Keepers?" I ask.

"Yes," says Vanderhorst. "But only because the Botellinos have been fairly vocal online about recruiting new members. They're on our watchlist."

"They killed Romanovich's entire bloodline!" Julia belts out from the pit. "At least that's what he said. Making Brandi his slave was his revenge."

Brandi was branded to be his? I swallow down my rage. I always thought Julia marked her for herself. The man they call Nails would have treated Brandi far worse than Narcissismo treated me. And he likely would have flaunted it too, ensuring

Brandi's parents were aware of what he was doing to their daughter.

I mean, do I know for certain that was his plan? No. But it is what I would do if I were an evil vampire hell-bent on revenge.

"So does Nails have her?" I ask Julia.

"Probably. But I told you, I haven't seen or heard anything since Houston. I swear it. Now, will you let me out of here? For the sake of an old friend?"

Nope. I strike the match, and Vanderhorst grabs my arm.

"Don't do it," he says.

"Five minutes ago she was auctioning your blood to a vicious leather-daddy softball team, and now you're defending her?"

"Not defending. The royal guards will be here any minute. Let them handle her and the barkeep. They'll get a trial and be punished—the right way."

I hate that idea! Stupid! But perhaps he has a point. It is time to let go of my old tyrant ways, the Mr. Nice ways. "Very well, but I want your word she will not be let off easy."

"I promise," says Vanderhorst.

"Today's your lucky day, Julia!" I call out. "You get to live."

"Don't leave me here!" she yells. "Let me out!"

I ignore her and exit the back room with Vanderhorst behind me, but as we pass the closet, I realize I have another loose thread. *Liza.*

I go to the closet where Pike is now crammed inside with a dead limp body.

I look at Vanderhorst to my side and quirk a brow. "Mr. By-the-Book, huh?"

"What? That was a legal kill." He shrugs innocently.

I suppose he's right. It's lawful to drink pedos, murderers, and rapists, who are generally very spicy. In my defense, I was also spicy, but none of those. I was merely evil. All right, fine! I murdered a few people. And perhaps many handfuls of vampires. But they all had it coming.

I turn my attention to Pike. "I am going to ask you one time only. Did you see a blonde in pink pajamas come through here earlier? She would have been traveling with a group of guards looking for Vanderhorst or my friend Brandi."

"No. I only saw him." Pike glances at Vanderhorst. "I swear it."

"If you are lying, I will return and take off your other ear. And by ear, I mean your belly button followed by—by something you don't need to survive but will cause you great public humiliation to lose."

Vanderhorst gives me a look.

"I'm rusty, okay? I've been watching *Sesame Street* the last five years."

"Fair point," Vanderhorst replies.

"Pike, are you sure?" I ask.

"Yes. Yes!"

"All right. The king's guards will be here shortly to free you." I slam the door shut, feeling proud of myself. I didn't dust him. I wanted to. I should have. But I didn't. I turned over a new leaf today.

Vanderhorst and I leave the Randy Unicorn. I stop just outside, feeling a niggling of doubt creeping into my stomach. "Are you sure we shouldn't…?" I point back inside and make an explosion motion with my hands.

"No. We will do this the right way." Vanderhorst lifts his chin.

"But I told Julia who you really are. I really should crush her sku—"

"No," Vanderhorst insists. "She will get what is coming to her, and no one will believe her anyway. She has no credibility in our world."

True. I nod in compliance. "So where do you think I will find Nails?" I ask.

"My best guess is that he's heading to the Botellinos'."

I give it some thought and agree. If I were a sadistic evil vampire out for revenge, I would take Brandi to her parents' house, subdue the family, and then execute her right in front of them. I would then do away with everyone in some sort of torturous, maniacal way. If we're talking Nails, he'll be getting out his favorite spike. "Do you have the Botellinos' address?"

Vanderhorst frowns. "Not on me, no. But you are going to Cincinnati."

"Why?"

"Nothing has changed, Nice. You must pay for your crimes."

Fucking Vanderhorst. "I saved you. I could have dusted you right there in that room and used what I know to overthrow Freddy."

"It does not erase what you did to Miriam, to me, to Stella. They are heartbroken. Did you know that? Did you!" He raises his voice. "Everyone adored you, and you screwed us."

The ache in my heart grows stronger. "I know what I did was not...the way of a man. It was underhanded and cruel. And I am not arguing with you; I should and will pay for my crimes, but I made a vow to protect Brandi. I must help her."

I know Vanderhorst better than I know anyone. His shrugged brows and crimped lips are a sign of reluctant surrender.

I add, "I vow I will go straight to Cincinnati once I have found her."

"You expect me to trust you? You, Mr. Nice?"

"I am not that man anymore. And if you want proof, then look at my actions today."

"Fine." He growls. "I will give you this one chance to prove yourself, but if you do not return to Cincinnati in two days, I will send the guards after you myself. I will petition to revoke your right to a trial and have you entombed, as originally planned."

I am strangely honored. Vanderhorst is a man who's vowed to destroy me as many times as I have him. That he is giving me his trust means something. "Thank you."

"Don't let me down, Nice."

"Steviuus," I correct. "Or Racker if you must. Mr. Sweet is also fine, but Mr. Nice is dead."

He stares for a long moment. "I want to believe that. But I will never call you Mr. Sweet. It is entirely preposterous."

"Then Steviuus."

He claps me on the shoulder, just like a father would to his son. "Make us proud, Steviuus."

I nod. And as I do, something to the side of the bar's front door catches my eye. It is a trash can. Sticking out from under the lid is a swatch of hot pink satin fabric.

I push Vanderhorst out of the way and throw the lid to the ground.

I stare down into the silver metal container filled with a pile of dust and some pink fabric. I pluck the garment from the ashes and hold it up.

No. No. No. It is Liza's pajamas.

The rage inside me is unlike anything I have ever known. *She was good. She was kind.* If I were capable of crying, I would. But I am an ancient, deadly vampire. We do not cry. We take revenge.

"What is that?" Vanderhorst asks, looking at the dirty pink shirt.

"They dusted my friend and the guards." I shove Liza's top at Vanderhorst. "Hold this." I kick down the bar's door and storm inside. I pull the book of matches from my pocket and go to the back room, where I light one up. "See you in hell."

I drop the match in the pit, and Julia screams. I do not bother to warn any of the patrons. If they are here, they are accomplices. They stood by and did nothing while Liza was murdered.

I exit the building as it goes up in flames. I hold the door handle so no one can leave.

Vanderhorst watches but doesn't say a word. For once, he is not judging.

CHAPTER TWENTY-THREE

I cannot believe Liza is gone. I only knew her a short time, but she was a friend who showed me another way. And that group of nasty, useless bloodsuckers took her life. Not fair that vampires like Larry Wiener Face, Pike the Pecker, and Julia the…the, well, whatever her handle was, should live on.

The world is a far better place without them.

As for Liza, I can only hope that she knows how much she will be missed.

I sigh as the private jet approaches the airport near Springfield, Missouri, around four in the morning. Vanderhorst volunteered to accompany me, but I declined and accepted the help of a handful of guards instead. If anything happened to Vanderhorst, Miriam and Stella would be lost.

"All right, men," I say as the plane prepares for landing, "the Botellino compound may have booby traps around the perimeter. Cameras, too. We must move carefully while hurrying to beat the sunrise." Vampires are weakened by the sun, but also the night will give us the best cover.

I continue, "As you're aware, we are unwelcome on their property. If Nails is already there, he has taken the family as prisoners, so that makes the situation more difficult. We have to rescue humans who may very well turn around and attempt to kill us." Our first task is to get inside the compound to assess the situation. If all is well, I simply need to ensure Brandi is all right. We will then have to hunt down Nails. If he hasn't attacked these people, he will.

If they are prisoners, we will dust Nails and whoever else he's brought along. I can only hope that Brandi and her family are all still alive. Nails never goes for the quick kill. *Nails likes to drain them slowly.* But this is about revenge for him.

Just before dawn, we arrive to the compound in two SUVs we arranged to have waiting at the airport. The property is about forty minutes from the small airport, surrounded by farms. We only have satellite images to go by, but it appears there is a house with a large barn in the back and two other outbuildings. A chain-link fence surrounds the perimeter, and there is only one way in—the long dirt driveway leading to the front of the house.

I zip up the black hoodie one of the guards gave me. They are dressed in black, their faces covered. Each came armed with both real bullets and choco-late-covered ones. I do not need a weapon. *I am one.*

I decide I'll take the front of the property, using

the driveway access, since I am the fastest. The team of guards will cut a hole in the fence and come around from the rear of the property. I will inspect the house. They will check out the other buildings. Once we assess, we will make our move.

I stand in the dark near the mailbox and stare down the long dirt road leading to the house. The muggy morning air smells of manure and fertilizers. The night is still, and the animals are quiet. I hear nothing coming from the direction of the house.

Spooky. Of course, I have been in far more dangerous situations, but this feels harrowing. I do not know what I will find here. Brandi and her family could be dead. And then what? What will I do?

I never had the chance to tell her how I feel. Or kiss her. I should've done it that night at the charity ball. I should have danced with her until the sun came up, but no. I took Liza outside to talk her into turning me. Then Brandi saw us and assumed the worst—I'd broken my promise to tell Liza the truth, that I was attempting to seduce her.

I can only hope I'll get the chance to make things right. And kiss her. Fine, and make sweet, sweet love to her. *The Mr. Sweet way.*

My phone vibrates in my jeans pocket. It's the signal. Time to move. I whoosh out a breath and get to it, running straight down the road until I get to a large tree at the side of the house. I wait a moment so the others can traverse the terrain in the back. They will give the signal once they are in position.

I wait. And I wait. And then I wait some more. But no signal.

Well, that's not good. I decide to check things out and head around the side of the house toward the barn out back. One of the men should be there now, preparing to enter.

No one.

Where did they go? I lift my nose into the air and draw a sharp breath through my nose. The smell is faint, but it is there. Ashes.

Jesus. What sorts of people live here? Apparently, people who are good at making traps and killing vampires. *Poor guards.* I didn't know them, but I am a good guy now. I have to at least pretend I care.

I guess I am on my own now. I decide that sneaking around the perimeter of the house is a very bad idea. The grounds seem well protected. I must go for the least obvious entry. The house. The front door. A vampire coming to attack would try a window. Or sneak in through the back of the property. *That was probably a stupid idea.* But not many would be so bold as to rush the front door.

I return to the front of the house. All is quiet, but if the guards set off traps, I must assume the people, or unwelcome vampires, inside have been alerted to a presence. I must be prepared for anything. Strike hard. Strike fast.

I hit the ground running and push the full force of my body into the front door. At impact I bounce right off and fly backward, landing on my ass with a thud. *Ouch!*

I sit up. I didn't even make a dent in the door. What's it made of? I rub my shoulder. If they didn't know I was here, they do now.

"Get up. Slowly." I hear a deep voice behind me. "And don't try anything. I've got a nice chocolate-coated arrow pointed at your head."

No winning. This plan needs a do-over.

I get to my feet, keeping my hands elevated. When I turn my head, I see an older man in overalls, with Brandi's large brown eyes, pointing a crossbow at me.

"Move!" he barks. "I'm taking you to the barn with the other leeches."

"So I take it Romanovich does not have your family prisoner, then?" I ask.

The man laughs. "You think your boss can best the Botellinos?"

"He is not my boss. I came to check on your family and to take him out."

"Yeah, sure. Get marching." Floodlights come on all around the compound. They were definitely prepared for intruders.

I start walking toward the barn. "And my men? Are any still alive?"

"'Fraid not. Spikes got 'em."

"Impressive. Oh, I mean, how very sad." I keep forgetting I am a good vampire now.

We get to the barn door, and he has me slide it open. Inside, the floor is covered in hay, and the place smells like animal dung. Lovely.

We go inside, and he marches me toward the back. Behind a wall of hay bales is a large steel cage. Puffy red eyes stare back at me.

"Brandi?"

"Racker?" She hops to her feet.

I turn toward her father. "What is the meaning of this? You cannot use your daughter as bait. Nails will come for you, and he won't be easy to best. She must be able to defend herself. Or run."

"Over here, idiot," says a familiar male voice.

I turn my head. There is another cage with a pale puny man inside. He has a large nose, and his brown eyes are too big for his head. He reminds me of a nerdy owl, but I know better than to judge a vampire book by its cover. This one is a mean little bugger. *Nails.*

I look at Brandi's father. "I'm pleased to see him in a cage, but why is your daughter locked up?" The rage begins to build inside me. She is mine to protect and has been since the day I saved her life. I do not like seeing her treated like an animal.

The man refuses to answer and opens the door to Nails's cage. "Get in."

"Can't I be with her?" I ask.

"In!" the man yells.

I am about to make a move when I notice we are not alone. There are men in the rafters all around us, pointing their crossbows in our direction.

"We need to have a discussion about your parents' hospitality," I say to Brandi.

I go inside the cage, and the door clanks behind me. I snarl at Nails.

"I'll be back at noon for the vampire roast," Brandi's dad says to the men up top. "Going to get some rest."

I look across at Brandi's cage. I am glad to see her alive, but I had not expected this. "Why are you caged?"

She sighs and looks down at the hay-covered floor. "Because my parents hate vampires. They kill vampires."

"Yes, but you are…you are…" I notice something is different about her. There's a sheen to her tan skin. She does not smell human. *No. Nooooo…* She looks lovely, of course, but someone touched her. Someone fed her their blood. Someone killed her and turned her against her will. They will pay! "When did this happen? Who turned you?"

"Julia," Brandi says quietly. "The night I rescued you."

I frown with confusion. "But you said…you said the police showed up and then this clown." I point to Nails.

She shakes her head. "I lied. I didn't want to make you feel bad. Julia had already beat me pretty badly before you found me in the shower. She forced me to drink some of her blood to heal and stop the bleeding before Romanovich showed up.

Then you came and helped me escape, but I couldn't leave you there. I found a big rock outside and went back in, to find Julia drinking you to death. I hit her in the head, but that only made her mad. She slammed me against the wall. I think I blacked out for a minute. When I woke up, the police were there, fighting that jerk." She points to Nails.

"Careful, woman. I will rip out your tongue," Nails snarls.

I turn, punch him in the face, and he falls over. Out like a light.

"Continue, Brandi." I dip my head.

Her eyes go wide. "You're strong. You're a vampire again. How?"

"Never mind that. Finish, please."

"Not much else to tell. I started dragging you out the back but didn't get very far. My head hurt so bad, and I couldn't see straight. You came to for a few minutes, groggy and bleeding, but we made it to that park together and collapsed. I woke up about an hour later. Dead. Changed. Whatever. You woke shortly after."

"Why didn't you tell me?" And how come I didn't notice she was a vampire?

"I'm sorry I didn't tell you." Brandi shakes her head with despair, tears rolling from her eyes. "I don't know. I guess, I just…I was trying to process it. I had no idea what to do. I mean, look around." She waves toward the men keeping guard over us. "I knew they'd disown me and never let me see my little sister again. But I never expected them to want to kill me."

Now I understand why she did not want to return home right away and why she wanted someone by her side when the time came. She feared how her parents would react.

"You should have said something," I scold. I could have been a source of comfort.

"I couldn't say it out loud. Then you told me about your situation, and I thought if I said anything, you would just try to get me to turn you."

"You wouldn't have done it," I conclude.

"No. Never. Well…that's what I thought at first, but then," she sighs, "I really started liking you, Racker. I promised myself that if you proved you could be a good man, an honest man, I would turn you. I'd save you if no one else stepped up."

All along I had the solution right next to me. Brandi. And of course, I couldn't tell she was a vampire. I'd lost my mojo, and she was very good at concealing it—unlike Liza. *Oh, Liza. Such a terrible vampire.* But such a nice person.

Anyway, I should have caught on to Brandi's secret. She kept picking at her food, and I never actually saw her eat a real meal.

"Liza knew, didn't she?"

Brandi nods.

When I told Liza about my vampire-hating girlfriend, Liza gave me a strange look. She knew all along that Brandi was a vampire. That's why she took us to the ball. She wanted Brandi to see that vampires could be good, do good. And of course, being the honorable woman that she was, Liza never gave away Brandi's secret.

"I am very sorry you felt you couldn't trust me," I say. "I would have helped you adjust or figure things out."

"Would you have?"

I give it some thought. "No, probably not." I had been too caught up in my own selfish needs. "I would have helped you speak with your parents though."

"Yeah, well, a lot of good that would have done. They threw me in here the minute I told them. They won't even let me see my little sister." The tears start coming again. I cannot bear to see Brandi like this. She's lost everything. On the other hand, I would not feel too bad about losing a family such as this. *They're a bit much.*

"I have a solution," I say. "We will tell them about the cure and take you to Cincinnati. They can come if they like to ensure you follow through."

"I already told them I planned to take the cure, but they'll never let me out of here. They think everything that comes out of a vampire's mouth is a lie."

They have a point. My mind scrambles, searching for a solution. I have been in many predicaments throughout my existence. Some I have fought my way through, but most I bullshitted through. This feels like a situation that calls for something entirely different.

Honesty. That is what Liza would advise me.

I look up at one of the men. "Hey, you. Go get Brandi's father. I wish to speak with him."

"His name is Hugo," says Brandi.

Ah yes. Hugo and Katarina. "Go get Hugo. Tell him I have information he'll want."

I hope this works. Because if not, we are screwed.

CHAPTER TWENTY-FOUR

Two hours later, I hear from one of the men that Hugo is on his way. Guess he was in no hurry to hear what I have to say. Fine by me. I passed the time telling Brandi all I went through searching for her, about how I would have eventually turned back to a vampire, but Liza helped me speed things along. Brandi cried when I told her about Liza getting dusted and said nothing about me torching the bar.

"I'm glad you won't be dying of old age, but I'm not glad it's going to end like this," she says.

"All right, I'm a busy man. What is it you want?" Hugo says, finally arriving. He is freshly shaved and has on a clean pair of brown overalls.

"I want to tell you I am going to rape your eye socket!" Nails snarls from behind me. "Let me out of here."

"I told you to be quiet." I turn and punch him again. Nails falls over onto the floor. He had it coming.

"Mr. Botellino," I say, "I would like to make a trade. Your daughter's life for the vampire king."

"Racker?" Brandi says. "What are you doing?"

I ignore her. She will simply have to trust me.

"Yeah? And how do you propose to give him to me?" Hugo asks, his tone filled with smugness.

"He and I are close. I will simply call and ask for help. He will come and attempt to rescue me. When he does, you will take him. As for your daughter, she will be released, and you will not follow her or ever try to find her."

"If you and he are close, why do you want him dead?" Hugo asks.

"It is a very long story. Five entire books, actually. But the short answer is: He will come because he cannot help himself. Hero complex." I shrug.

"Racker, don't do this," Brandi says. "I don't want someone else dying in my place. Remember what I said before? Punches and wins?"

Ah yes. "You can't hijack someone else's life. And you get to live the life that's given to you. Take the punches with the wins." Blah, blah, blah.

"I already won," she adds. "I met you. That's enough for me."

"Sorry," I say, "but you're not done living yet. And if I must choose between his life and yours, I choose you."

"Shut up. We're having a conversation here. How many men will he come with?" Hugo asks.

"A lot. Which presents a grand opportunity for you to take out more vampires. And after you deal with them, more will come."

I can tell by the twinkle in his eyes that he likes the idea of killing as many vampires as possible.

"So do we have a deal?" I ask.

"Yes. But you and that guy stay. You'll die with your king."

I shrug. "Fair, I suppose, since I am double-crossing him."

Hugo nods.

"But you must let Brandi go first," I say. "She must FaceTime me from a safe location—the airport—so I can see she is genuinely there." They cannot bring their weapons into the airport, and she can fly anywhere she pleases. "Make sure she has what she needs to buy a ticket. And let her say goodbye to her sister."

"You're adding to the terms," Hugo says. "Not sure you're in a position to make demands like that."

"Killing the vampire king and putting a dent in his army is a big prize for you and your Keeper cult."

"We are not a cult. We are dedicated to cleansing the world of your kind, doing God's work to behead the army of Satan. We will not rest until every last one of you is purified by his glorious sunlight and burned alive. Then we will dance on your ashes under a full moon so you never rise again."

Yes, doesn't sound culty at all. "Well, if that sounds like a fun time to you, who I am I to argue? I never was a fan of vampires myself. We're pretty rotten. Well, except your daughter. You raised a truly beautiful and remarkable woman." How did they manage it? These people seem a little nuts.

Hugo winces with disgust. "My daughter is dead."

"Technically she still has a heartbeat, and after she takes the cure—if that's her desire—she will be human again." I look straight at her. "Whatever she chooses, I want her to know Liza showed me there was another way, but your daughter was the reason I took the other path. She was my motivation to change." It is true. Doing right felt like doing right by her. It made me feel good.

Brandi stares with adoring, but sad eyes.

I stare back, offering my own look of adoration. "I can say, with all honesty, I will die a happy man. To be looked at that way, by such a wonderful woman, is the best feeling in the world. Thank you." I dip my head at Brandi.

Nails starts to stir with a groan. I lean over and punch him. "You do not get to die happy," I growl. "You are a very bad man."

Hugo shakes his head. "You ready to do this?"

"Yes."

"Racker, no!" Brandi says.

"This is the only way one of us gets to live. And the deal is struck. Too late to back out now."

CHAPTER TWENTY-FIVE

Brandi is dragged from her cage, and I show no emotion. I do not wish for her last memory of me to include worry on my face.

She must remember me as I am now. Strong, protective, and fearless. Also, with thick waves of dark hair and smoldering bedroom eyes. At the very least she will have a good memory to pleasure herself to after I am gone.

An hour later, Hugo appears with his phone in hand. He shows me the screen. I see Brandi's face.

"Are you safe?" I ask, being as cold as I can so she stays calm. Meanwhile, my heart is in turmoil. I genuinely wish to tear these people to shreds to get to her and be by her side.

"Yes, I'm at the airport." She sniffles.

I can see from the activity in the background that she is. "Good. And you know where to go if you wish to get the cure, yes?"

Her lower lip quivers, and she pushes her messy chocolate-colored locks from her face. "Yes."

"I love you. Thought I would throw that out there in case you had any doubts." In fact, she is the first, I realize. The others, not that there were many, weren't really love. Miriam was right about that. But Brandi, I can say with all honesty that she has found her way into my heart. I place her above all else. "Goodbye."

Hugo ends the call. "You're a smooth-talking devil, aintcha? Time to call your friends. Number?"

I give it to him, and he dials. After a few rings, Vanderhorst's voice comes on. "What happened? Why aren't you on your way back?"

"Unfortunately," I say, "the guards were dusted, and now I'm cornered. I need your help."

"What happened?"

"I'll tell you when you get here. Just come. Quickly. I'm holed up in the barn at the Botellinos'."

Hugo ends the call. "This'd better work."

"It will."

Hugo grunts and leaves.

"You're really double-crossing our king?" Nails asks, slouched over in the corner.

I nod.

"I never liked him."

I raise my fist, and he goes to block it. "Okay. Okay. I'll stop talking."

"Good choice." Hey, I never said I planned to be a pacifist. Nails planned to enslave Brandi and torture her so her parents would suffer. He deserves much worse than a few fist poundings. "Why did the Botellinos go after your coven anyway?"

"I'd rather not say. Long story."

"We've got about four or five hours until Vanderhorst arrives." And I need to keep my mind off the fact that I will never see Brandi again.

"I got involved with a family member. It was years ago, but Hugo didn't take it well."

Oh. I wonder who Nails nailed. "Well, good job. Next time, try sticking to your own species."

"You're one to talk. And for the record, she came on to me."

As if it matters now. "Hope she was worth it."

"I'd do it all over again if I had the chance."

I suppose I understand. I would trade anything for one night with Brandi. "I'm going to get some rest. Things will get interesting once the vampire army shows up."

"You really think the king will come?"

"Yes." And I hope he forgives me. Miriam and Stella will not be happy either. But sometimes a vampire must be a little evil to do good.

ৡৣ ৶

It is almost midnight by the time I wake. Hugo's armed men are hiding throughout the barn. I can hardly hear them breathing, they are well trained, but I know they are there, and more are outside, waiting to ambush Vanderhorst.

I cannot believe how long I slept. Vampires do not have to sleep, but it helps to keep our axes sharp. And after everything I've been through, I needed it.

Especially since Vanderhorst hasn't shown. Why not? Why hasn't he answered my plea for help?

Several hours pass and still nothing.

By dawn, I am beginning to think I overplayed my hand. Vanderhorst doesn't care if I live or die. *I was a fool to think otherwise.*

In a way, I'm glad he didn't come. I do not wish Miriam and Stella to be left without a protector. Not that Freddy would allow that, but it is not the same as having Michael around. Love him or hate him, he is an excellent fighter when he's not too busy overthinking things. It is rumored that Vanderhorst's maker had to teach him to completely turn off his emotions in order to fight in the Great War. Once he did, he became a killing machine. A legendary assassin. The Executioner.

Later, he'd regain his emotions and become Mr. Morality again. *Blech!* The irony is that Miriam loves both sides of him. Or perhaps it is a blessing. No matter if he is the apex predator or pussy-whipped husband, she is down with it.

Love is blind. It is also life changing, and I had a taste for a few precious moments thanks to Brandi.

I watch with dread as the sun comes up and the morning rays push through the cracks in the barn's siding. Hugo, who left hours ago to get more sleep, returns with chains.

"I'm flattered, Hugo, but I am already taken," I say.

"Shut up." He looks upset—red face, flat lips,

pulsing jaw. "Your friends didn't come, and if they do, we'll be ready, but there's no point in keeping you two animals alive."

"What about your daughter?" I ask, hoping she is far enough away that they cannot nab her again. The deal with her father obviously fell through. Perhaps she is off on some beach or maybe robbing a bank with her new vampire skills—something fun and exciting like that.

"She's gone, but we'll find her," he says.

Doubtful. Brandi is smarter than the lot of them.

Hugo hooks the cage up to the chains and then attaches them to a horse outside. Well, not the actual horse. It's wearing a yoke.

Our cage is dragged outside behind the barn to a clearing where a large group has gathered. Men, women, and even a few children. Everyone is dressed like they are ready for a barn dance. Crisp white shirts, pressed pants, and petticoat frocks.

"I feel so special," I say. "Are you all here to watch the end of the glorious Mr. Nice? Let the record show that I changed my name to Mr. Sweet, and I was not a bat-shit crazy vampire in the end."

The crowd mumbles among themselves.

I notice Nails staring through the bars. I follow his gaze to a woman in her late forties, early fifties, standing at the back of the crowd. She has Brandi's round face and pouty lips. Same dark hair, too.

My gaze toggles between the two. Forlorn woman. Nails. Forlorn woman. Nails.

"You just had to fang the cult leader's wife, didn't you?" I shake my head. "You really are an idiot, Nails."

He stares at her, as if reaching with his eyes and emotions. "She came on to me. We belonged to the same bowling league."

I flash him a look. Never struck me as a bowler. But I guess that's the thing about vampires, especially the evil ones. They're unpredictable. I know from personal experience that my erratic, irrational behavior scared the hell out of everyone. People and vampires want to know the rules are consistent and fair. When they're not, it sparks fear.

Wait. That's it.

I push myself against the bars as Hugo and his men ready the gas cans for the grand cook-off. "Hugo! I appreciate you bringing some of my vampire friends to watch my execution! Very kind not to let us die in the company of only humans."

He glances my way but ignores me and continues with the setup, including unloading firewood from a crate.

"Joe! So nice to see you. How's the broken fang?" I say to a young man in the front of the group, wearing a white cowboy hat.

The young man looks around, wondering who I'm talking to.

"Why did you join this cult?" I ask "Joe." "You were so good at the whole throat-ripping thing."

Joe's eyes toggle back and forth. "I don't know you."

"Really now? You're going to pretend you didn't come to my fangtastic party the other night with Bob?" I look at another man next to him.

"Stop. I know what you're doing," says Hugo. "No one here is a vampire."

"Well, not anymore," I say. "But with so many vampires having taken the cure, ex-vampires are everywhere."

"If anyone here was ever an unholy creature, I would know. And there is no cure for an unholy soul." Hugo continues placing wood around our cage.

"But your wife doesn't agree," I say. "Isn't that right? She has a thing for Nails here."

From the tightness in his body, I know that pushed his buttons. *Excellent.*

"Why is it that you are such a hater and your wife is such a lover?" I ask.

"You shut up, blood sucker. Foul demon! Everyone knows your kind can't be trusted." Hugo throws his arms in the air and starts to chant. It's in Latin.

I wonder if he knows he's asking the God of Scrotums for a new backhoe.

The downside of using the internet for translations.

"Perhaps I cannot be trusted," I say, "but I'm not the one who wanted to burn his daughter alive. All because she was attacked by a vampire while trying to save a man's life. It wasn't her fault she turned. In fact, she was doing exactly what you taught her to do. Help others. Defend them from 'the monsters.' And that is precisely what she did. She protected an unconscious man, and she paid the price for trying to make you proud. But you turned your back on her. Didn't you? Just like you would turn your back on every person here, including Joe and Bob. Even if they're human now."

"I was never a vampire. And my name is Steve. Not Joe," says the guy.

I wink at him. "Your secret is safe with no one."

He shakes his head.

Meanwhile the others start speaking amongst themselves. They are starting to see that their leader might not be worth following if he has no mercy for his flock. Especially if they are "injured" in the line of duty.

I clear my throat and address the crowd, whose expressions are increasingly uncomfortable. "Do you all honestly believe that Katarina would fall in love with a vampire if Hugo's hate wasn't so toxic? Because, trust me, I know. I was once the most toxic creature on the planet. I drove everyone away.

"I would kill anyone, say anything, and do anything if it pleased me. I didn't care. Until one day, I became human again, and Hugo's daughter showed me kindness. Yes, I am the man she helped. And yes, I am a vampire again. But that doesn't change how her goodness has made a difference in this world. Yet her own father won't acknowledge her or look her in the eyes. And he calls me a demon?"

The quiet murmurs of the crowd turn into impassioned debates. Suddenly, Hugo is yelling, and they are yelling back.

There are questions around why his wife betrayed him, why he refused to help Brandi. No one likes the fact that if they were somehow turned while serving his cause, he would burn them alive. Then the yelling starts.

Hugo is a hypocrite!

This is not what we signed up for!

Suddenly, the mob turns angry, and fights break out.

Katarina marches over and pops open the cage. "Nails, run! I will see you in our secret place."

"I am not leaving here without you," he says and flings her over his shoulder before zipping away.

So sweet, I think and step outside as they all start to brawl amongst themselves. I don't bother coming to Hugo's defense when he's thrown to the ground. "Reap what you sow, friend."

I am about to take off when five cop cars pull up, sirens blazing.

What the…

Vanderhorst hops from the back of the first car. "Steviuus!"

"Vanderhorst? What's going on?"

Everyone stops their fighting, and the officers start throwing people to the ground, handcuffing them. Hugo is the first to be arrested.

"What the hell do you think is going on?" Vanderhorst snaps.

My head whips around. "You called the police? The actual police?" Very smart. Hugo's people would attack vampires, no problem. But human police? Not likely. And to the authorities, I am just another law-abiding citizen in need of assistance in a hostage situation.

Vanderhorst gives me a look. "I knew this was a trap. I knew you were setting me up. I just don't know why."

See, friends, here's the thing about life; you can change your colors, you can change your heart, but changing people's minds? Well, that is another story.

Once you lose a person's trust, it can take an eternity to get it back. They will always doubt you. They will always question your motives.

This is why it is paramount to believe in yourself. Know who you are. Do not let the world dictate. Because, at the end of the day, you cannot control what others think. *Ah, but you can use it to your advantage.* I was counting on Vanderhorst not trusting me and taking the appropriate precautions. He did not let me down.

My grin stretches ear to ear. "It wasn't a trap. Nor did I set you up. I simply knew that you will never change. Even if I have."

I walk off, lifting my chin.

"Nice! You still made a promise! I expect you to be in Cincinnati!" Vanderhorst calls out.

"I will be there."

CHAPTER TWENTY-SIX

I was able to retrieve my phone before leaving the compound, but when I attempt to reach Brandi, the number is no longer active. I assume she ditched her cell so she could not be tracked.

I just hope the vampire nation will do what it always does, gossip like mad, and word will reach her that I am safe and sound. *And behind bars.* The same goes for her father and his cult members. I was obliged to make a statement to the authorities before my departure from Missouri, but I do not know if I will return for the trials. If there are any. Hugo and his people might tell the police the truth, in which case they will be committed.

It's where they belong anyway. *And far better than this place.* I look around the drab gray cell located in the basement below vampire headquarters. Ironically, this is where it all began—my journey to reclaim my humanity. The laboratory is just down the hall and is the very spot where I took the cure.

"You ready?" One of the guards appears at the door.

"I am." I have been up all night preparing. Today the charges against me will be read, and I will make my plea. After that, there will be a trial unless the king decides I do not deserve one. Either way, I do not expect to walk away a free man.

"Just one guard, huh?" I say.

"I'm really more of an escort. If you wanted to run, you would have, and I'm not about to fight you." He leans in. "I heard you drank Freddy Vanderhorst's blood. Impressive."

I shrug. To my surprise, I simply do not care how powerful I am any more. It will not get me what I want.

The guard leads me to the elevator, and we step inside. He hits the button for the ground floor. "Where are we going?" I ask.

"The great hall."

That can only mean one thing. Many have come to witness the proceeding.

The doors slide open, and we are greeted by a crowd of vampires, many of the faces familiar. Everyone is bobbing their head back and forth, trying to get a look at me.

"Wow. He really does look sexy."

"I'm so taking the cure now. I want a do-over too."

"I heard he's the third-strongest vampire in the world now."

"Mmmm…I want me some Mr. Sweet."

The old me would have soaked it up, but the new me ignores them all. I only want to see Brandi again. And to apologize to Miriam. I suppose Stella and Michael, too.

I enter the great hall, which is packed tight. Up on the platform, sitting at a table, is Freddy Vanderhorst and Gretta, his wife. Acting king and queen of all vampires.

I take my seat in front of them below, the room to my back. I have no lawyer. I did not want one.

One of the guards calls the room to attention. That's when I notice Miriam, Stella, and Vanderhorst seated in the front to my right. I did not expect them to come.

The room quiets, and Freddy stands to address the crowd.

It is uncanny how he has mastered being his brother. The stern gaze in his dark eyes. The smug demeanor.

I think he is very brave to allow a public hearing for me. He and his brother know I could use the forum to disclose their secret.

"Mr. Nice, you are accused of a multitude of crimes by nearly every person in this room. As is the law, we will read the charges one by one, and then you will have the opportunity to make a plea for each. Do you understand?"

I turn my head and look at all the faces. "All of them? They all filed complaints?"

Freddy shrugs. "They heard you were going to be put on trial and decided to pile on. Guess you've got a few centuries to answer for."

I swallow a lump in my throat. This is going to

be interesting.

"Racker!" I hear Brandi's sweet voice echo from the back of the room.

I turn my head to see her standing in a lovely pink dress, her long dark hair pinned up, her cheeks flushed. My insides tighten, my cold heart warms. I wasn't sure I'd ever see her again. *And she just had to show up now? Damn my luck.*

I give her an awkward wave.

"Ma'am, please be seated," Freddy says.

Brandi comes forward to the bench behind me. "Move!" She pushes everyone over with her ass and sits.

Wonderful. Now she won't miss a word. I face forward.

Freddy gives the nod to the clerk, who comes over with a book as thick as my arm.

"Eh-hem. In the case of…of…well, pretty much everyone versus Mr. Nice—"

"Excuse me," I say. "I no longer go by that name. I am Steviuus Nicephorus Racker."

The clerk blinks. "Um, in the case of everyone versus Mr. Racker, formally known as Mr. Nice, I hereby read the following charges: Animal cruelty, arson, attempted murder, attempted treason, burglary, disfiguring a vampire with his own genitals, dismembering a member of the royal guard, dismembering a vampire official, three hundred counts of illegal dusting, impersonating a celebrity…

෧ඁ ෧ඁ

Five hours later…

"And, last but not least," says the clerk with a yawn, "five counts of zoning violations."

I have not dared to look at Brandi this entire time. I am certain that she could never love me now. I was quite the ambitious evil vampire. Though, I will say, ninety percent of the acts I committed were justified or they happened long, long ago. Times were different then. *Some of these items weren't even crimes yet.*

The clerk slaps the book closed and looks at the glossy-eyed king. "And that concludes the last ten years. Shall we take a break, sir, before we get to the next decade?"

Oh. I finally turn and look at Brandi, who doesn't return my gaze. Her eyes are locked straight ahead, her pouty lips puckered tightly. She is in shock. On the bright side, she is still here. That could be a positive sign?

Who am I kidding? I am doomed. I look the other way toward my family—ex-family. Miriam shakes her head at me. I know what she must think. How could she ever have let me in her home? Trusted me? And she would be right. She shouldn't have, and making her sit through all this is not what I want. It's pouring salt in her wounds. Nor does Brandi need to hear more and wonder what is the matter with her for thinking she might want to be with such a bad, evil, cruel man.

I stand. "In the interest of saving everyone time, I ask that we skip the rest of the reading. I plead guilty to all of it. Well, except the animal cruelty part. The horses, ducks, and other animals in my menagerie were never harmed when I had them painted red. I only used food coloring." It was a *Fanged Love* theme party. What can I say? "But I do not wish to put those I care for through more. Let us simply get on with sentencing and be done with it."

Freddy gives me a hard look. "I appreciate the gesture; however, don't you wish to say something in your defense? Or explain your behavior?"

I turn and look around at the faces in the room. Yes, I recall a few unpleasant interactions with some. However, most lined up to attend my legendary parties or to do my evil bidding because they wished to have a powerful vampire on their side.

And of course they all forget that I ended the Great Coup, when our entire leadership council was gutted and everything vampires had worked to build over three centuries—prosperous businesses, integration in the human world, an end to societal wars and turf disputes—was about to be taken away by a group of vampires led by Cluentius Boethius, Michael's maker. I killed him. War over. Thousands of lives saved. Did I commit a few crimes during that time, too? Maybe. But they all benefited from it.

Bottom line, the world needs evil vampires, but

no one wants to admit it. And, frankly, I'm tired of playing the role. I got no appreciation.

"No, I do not wish to say anything." I pause. "Well, except." I turn to face Miriam, Michael, and Stella. "Thank you for taking me into your home. I am truly sorry for any pain I caused you. It was an honor being part of your family; even if Vanderhorst is an annoying fool, he was a very good father. And Miriam, you are a phenomenal mother. The way you care for everyone around you, including your community, is genuinely inspiring. And Stella, you are the bravest little girl I have ever known." It is not easy being a half-vampire child who doesn't fit in anywhere.

I turn to Brandi, who still refuses to look at me. "I am very sorry you had to hear all this, Brandi. I know this is not what you needed after everything you have been through. But thank you for giving me a reason to change my ways and learn what it truly means to be a man. I will always love you."

I face the front of the room, chin held high.

"Take him back to his cell," Freddy says to the guard. "We will call him back once we have decided his punishment."

I leave the great hall unsure of what lies ahead. I only know that a small part of me feels good to close this long chapter of my existence. Mr. Nice is no more. The world now knows the real me. They can take it or leave it. But I stand tall. And ready for entombment.

CHAPTER TWENTY-SEVEN

I pace my cell for what feels like a week. Perhaps it has been. There is no light down here. I have no phone. No one has come to see me or give word on the status of my sentencing.

With each and every minute that ticks by, my despair grows. I thought this was going to be fairly simple. Entombment. Just as Vanderhorst proposed as part of our agreement.

But this delay could mean they are pushing for death. *If I were the king, I would.* It serves no purpose having a powerful vampire like me roaming about. It's like I said before, friends. Our world is made up of two kinds of vampires. Those who obey the laws, and those who don't. Me? I used to be a "don't" but now fall somewhere in the middle. I do not care for anarchy and chaos, but some of the old ways make sense. For example, if a vampire comes after the people I care about, there will be no trial. There will be no discussions. I will drop the match.

"Sir?" The guard shows up. "They're ready for you."

I swallow down the grit in my throat. "Is she still here?" I ask.

"Who?"

"That woman in the pink dress."

His eyes light up with lust. "Brandi Botellino? Oh yeaaah, she's still here."

I narrow my eyes.

"Yes, sir." He clears his throat. "She is still here."

"Ask her to leave. I do not wish her to see more." It is time for her to get on with her life. She should take the cure, be happy, live free.

"I don't think that's going to happen."

"Why? What have they done to her?" I grab the bars of my cell.

"Nothing. She's fine. But…why don't you let her explain?"

I am confused. What could she possibly have to explain?

I follow the guard back up to the great hall. To my surprise it is even more packed than before. Standing room only. I see many faces from the past. Evil vampires, really, really evil vampires, and some good ones. Everyone is quiet, and a deep chill runs through my bones. This does not look good.

I walk to the front of the room, and this time I see Brandi sitting next to Miriam, holding hands. *Wow. I did not see that coming.*

"Mr. Racker, please remain standing for sentencing," says the clerk.

Freddy stands, too, and gives me a stern look. I bet he's enjoying this. Well, actually, it would be

Michael who is savoring the moment. Revenge is his.

"Steviuus Nicephorus Racker, after much debate and testimony from members of the community, including my own brother, we were compelled to reconsider the harshness of the applicable punishment. You are hereby sentenced to one hundred years of community service as our general of the army."

Huh?

He continues, "I will be vacating my throne soon, and as we reestablish the prior system of leadership councils, we will require someone with a very firm hand to keep the order. Someone who is loyal and willing to protect those around him but also knows all the tricks and treachery our kind is capable of. Someone who understands the complexities of our society. And since I do not know another vampire who scares the hell out of everyone quite like you, I am confident you are just what our vampire nations need at this critical juncture."

My mouth flaps. I am speechless.

"In addition," he goes on, "you will promise to spend holidays with your family and cease all rivalries with me." He means his brother, Michael. "You understand that you are ineligible for the cure until your sentence is served." Freddy exhales sharply. "Do you accept these terms?"

I nod dumbly.

"Good. This hearing is adjourned. Refreshments

are in the lobby, including free ice cream. Our special today is bloody berry in our newly remodeled store." The headquarters doubles as an ice-cream company. Did I fail to mention that? Everyone must have a cover story in the human world. Ice-cream mogul is the king's.

The room starts to empty, but I am left glued to the floor, my feet unable to move.

"Racker?" Brandi comes up. "Are you all right?"

I blink. "I don't understand what just happened."

She stands in front of me. "I think it's pretty obvious, don't you?"

I shake my head. "How am I still alive right now? I thought for certain they were going to dust me."

"Your family came to your rescue."

I frown just as Miriam, Michael, and Stella walk up.

"I want to see you Sunday for dinner," says Miriam and walks off. Stella trails behind her and sticks her tongue out at me, then smiles.

I look at Michael, who is standing beside Brandi. "What happened?" I ask him.

Michael claps me on the shoulder. "You could've hurt my family and thrown our people back into civil war. You didn't. Plus, your woman here put up a good fight. See you Sunday." He walks off to join the crowd outside.

I look down at Brandi. "What did you say?"

"I just told them about the man I recently met who almost died twice saving me."

"And they believed you?"

"There were witnesses to back me up. Remember the other women at Julia's? They showed up. So did a couple of the guys from my dad's compound. And then of course your mother told everyone how you swooped in and rescued her when some vampire was about to take her head off. And I guess there was that incident at that bar in Vegas—you saved the king's brother?"

Michael testified for me?

"The list of good deeds was not nearly as long as your rap sheet," Brandi says, "but it was pretty powerful stuff. Oh, and your mom, she's great. The two of us are going to get along really well, which is wonderful. Since you and I'll be getting married soon."

"Married?" I raise a brow.

"I'm guessing you want to sleep with me, and I already told you: I'm saving myself."

"You are being serious right now?" We haven't even kissed. "You want to be with a vampire who was just saved from death because he is notoriously evil?"

She steps in closer and bats her eyelashes. "I know who you are, Mr. Sweet. And he's the man I want to be with forever."

"You're not going to take the cure?"

"I think it's an option after you've served your

sentence—and if it's something we want to do together, provided they figure out a way to make it work on you and prevent you from turning into a baby. I don't think I could handle that."

I thread my fingers in the back of her hair and band my arm around her waist. "Can you handle this?" I lean down and press my mouth to her soft lips.

The rush is unlike anything I've ever known. Heat, energy, tingles in very sexual places. I suddenly understand what all the fuss is about. Falling in love with the perfect woman, your one true mate, is a drug like nothing else. Suddenly, I know the journey has ended. I am home. And I am so incredibly horny.

"Where's the nearest wedding chapel?"

CHAPTER TWENTY-EIGHT

Five weeks later, I am about to lie with my new wife. Brandi Racker. Or Mrs. Sweet as I call her in private. The ceremony was a quiet one at a local chapel in Phoenix. Family only. Michael was my worst best man—Miriam forced him to play the role, and he scowled the entire time. I think he misses having me as his adversary. Miriam cried through the entire ceremony. I do not know if they were tears of joy because I will never torment her marriage again, or because she was truly overjoyed for my happiness. Stella continued to be the mischievous defiant girl I adore. She will make a great leader someday.

As for the delay in our nuptial ceremony, and my constant need for very loose pants—Brandi's kisses are like no other—we had to put our own needs on hold following my trial.

I had not been aware at the time, but Brandi's little sister had been taken into Child Services' custody following Hugo's arrest. I simply assumed Katarina had gotten her. So did Brandi.

But a few days later, I managed to track down Nails and Katarina for my soon-to-be wife (so we could invite them to the wedding), and we discovered that Marigold was in custody.

Of course, we had to hire a lawyer, petition for Brandi to take custody, and then the real problems began.

Marigold, who is not much older than Stella, refused to come with us. She told the authorities that her sister is a vampire. And so is her fiancé. So, of course, Marigold was placed in psychiatric care.

Brandi was heartbroken. But I understood. The poor thing had just been abandoned by her mother and traded in for a vampire named Nails. Hugo had brainwashed Marigold to hate vampires, Brandi included. Her mother's departure was simply evidence to never trust our kind. Evil. It seemed that Hugo would have his slice of revenge after all.

Except that I am vampire man. Vampire on the outside. Man on the inside. And still just a little evil. I am willing to break the rules to protect those I love. Consequences be damned.

Oh, and also, I am now the second most powerful vampire in the world. General Racker. Has a very nice ring to it.

So I did what any loving man in power would do for his betrothed, and I stole Marigold. Then I took a page out of Liza's book and treated Marigold with kindness. I showed her the good a vampire could do for the world if they chose to. I brought her to Miriam's public library, introduced her to Stella, and took her to a Vampires for Caring meeting. She got to see some pretty extraordinary vampires. Some even have human spouses.

Marigold still clings to some rather strange ideas, such as vampires came from the devil, but I was simply honest. "I do not know where we came from. Just as humans do not." God? Aliens? Evolution? "All I can tell you is that we were human once. Some of us will be again. And everyone must choose how to live their lives. Whether it's eighty years or eight centuries. But it is our choice, and no one else's."

Brandi liked that answer.

Now Marigold seems to be settling in, cautious but curious about what her beloved sister has become and how we eat so many hot peppers in one sitting. I am confident that with time, Marigold will make up her own mind and see us as the family who will always be there for her.

That brings me to my point: We postponed the wedding until Marigold would be comfortable enough to stay with Miriam, Michael, and Stella for a few days.

I strip off my tux, put on my white robe, and open the tap to fill the sunken tub with hot water. I pour a little jalapeño oil in the water for Brandi's enjoyment. Soft Latin-techno plays over the surround system throughout the house so that we can hear it no matter what room we end up in.

"Seriously?" Panting, Brandi bursts into the master bath, still in her white lace wedding dress.

"This is your place?"

I smile. "Our place."

"But, but…why were you staying at your parents' house before?"

"Well, I could hardly fend for myself. I was only five."

"Very funny. You're over three hundred years old, and you look about twenty-five."

"I suppose I enjoyed living in a home versus a house. Now, anywhere we go, it will be home if you are with me. I have several other properties in—"

"Nope. No, thank you. I'm all done with change for a while. This place is perfect. Room for Marigold, the school is close by, and I don't think I'll ever tire of the view. That pool with the waterfall is amazing."

She doesn't know it yet, but she will learn after a few decades that the newness wears off. Material things only provide a small bit of comfort for immortals. "Houses, cars, jewelry, yachts, and private jets come and go. I have plenty of those. But there is only one you." I close the gap between us. "Your happiness is the only thing that matters."

"You say that now, but what happens in twenty, thirty, a hundred years? Will you still want me then?"

She doesn't get it, does she? "I have waited over three hundred years for you. Do you honestly think I will ever take you for granted?" I slide my hand to the back of her neck and kiss her hard because the time for words is over. I am a vampire of action. And she is going to get plenty of it.

I move my mouth over hers, and her lips are like rose petals made of seductive magic. Her soft body is a beacon to my possessive vampire male. Her face makes me forget any other woman exists.

I scoop her up and take her to the king-size bed in the other room, where I have placed fresh white linens with rose petals atop—well, I had one of my men do it, but it's the thought that counts. The curtains are open, exposing the balcony with a view of the city below. Candles flicker in the fireplace because, well, it's hot outside and a fire doesn't sound appealing. But she does. She is perfect. Our wedding was perfect. And I know sex will be perfect.

I lay her on the bed, caressing her with my loving gaze. She is so beautiful I hardly have the words to describe what she does to me. "I'm going to pound you into this mattress until it breaks, little virgin."

She laughs. "Wow. That sounds rough. How about we take it easy the first time? Save the pounding for the second round."

I strip off her clothing by ripping her wedding gown down the middle.

"Hey, I wanted to save that," she protests.

"I will buy you another."

I shed my robe, and her eyes go wide at the sight of my erection. "Oh crap. No wonder why you never had sex with a human woman."

I smile proudly. I am both a shower and a grower. Big just gets bigger. "I wasn't called Mr. Nice for nothing."

"Yeah, but...then shouldn't your name have been...Mr. Cockasauru—"

"Silence." I lay myself between her thighs, pinning her hands above her head. "No more words. Only moaning."

I thrust and then...feel our bodies melt into one. It is better than I could have imagined.

Sixty seconds later...

"Um..." Brandi holds the covers over her chest as I lay beside her, panting. "That was...um..."

"That's never happened before. I swear." It's the truth.

"Well, it didn't hurt as much as I thought. Guess the whole vampire-body thing has some perks."

I cannot believe this. I turn onto my side. "It is your fault. Weeks of teasing and kissing and strutting around in your sexy clothing."

"What? I wore jeans and whatever."

"Exactly. So enticing. If you want me to last longer, you're going to have to try harder. Be less...you know. Provocative and sexy."

She laughs and beams at me. "You really are funny. You know that?"

I smile. I love that she still looks at me even if I botched her first time. "I love you, Brandi."

"I love you, too. And I'm so happy to start this new life with you."

"I am pleased you say that, because it comes with many other perks." *Me for one. And also…*

"Oh!" Her big eyes light up. "What's that?"

"Your perk." Vampires might take forever to find their mates and fall in love, but they do not need much time to recuperate in the bedroom. "Now prepare yourself, woman. This is a onetime-only encore just for you." *Some kinky Mr. Nice-style lovemaking coming right up.* I feel she deserves to experience supreme lovemaking at its finest. After all, she is my one true love. I would do anything for her, including being perfectly nice.

THE END?

AUTHOR'S NOTE

Hello to all my vampire fans out there! I hope you enjoyed Mr. Sweet's journey! I like that he found his place in the world, while being just a tiny bit evil. Ha!

I don't have plans for more Librarian's Vampire Assistant books at the moment, but you can always check in here for possible updates:
www.mimijean.net/lva-series.html

Always best to subscribe to my fantastic, non-spammy newsletter for all the updates on upcoming releases:
www.mimijean.net/get-news-from-mimi.html

If you are looking for one of my coveted signed bookmarks for your collection, you know what to do!

STEP ONE: Email me at Mimi@mimijean.net

STEP TWO: Provide your complete shipping address with country (if you're outside of the US).

STEP THREE: If you LOVED this story and wrote a review, be sure to provide a link or screenshot. I will do my very best to include extra goodies. It is first ask, first get! (NOTE: I have a very limited supply of magnets this time around.)

STEP FOUR: Give me about 3–4 weeks to sign a mountain of swag. ☺

With Sweet Hugs,
Mimi

PS – Looking for the *Vampire Man* Playlist? LISTEN ON SPOTIFY

ACKNOWLEDGMENTS

A huge gushing thank-you to everyone who worked on and pitched in to make *Vampire Man* sparkle and shine! (Book #51! Woohoo!) Author Kylie Gilmore, Dali, Paul, Su, Stephanie, and Pauline.

Also, thank you to Susan Manson for the inspiration for Narcissimo's name (she came up with Narcissus on the fan group page)! It was a perfect fit for Nice's maker.

As always, huge hugs to my dudes for always being there, ready to pitch in with the never-ending work. I love you.

Big Hugs,
Mimi

ABOUT THE AUTHOR

MIMI JEAN PAMFILOFF is a *New York Times* bestselling author who's sold over one million books around the world. Although she obtained her MBA and worked for more than fifteen years in the corporate world, she believes that it's never too late to come out of the romance closet and follow your dreams.

Mimi lives with her Latin lover hubby, two pirates-in-training (their boys), and their three spunky dragons (really, just very tiny dogs with big attitudes) Snowy, Mini, and Mack, in the vampire-unfriendly state of Arizona.

She hopes to make you laugh when you need it most and continues to pray daily that leather pants will make a big comeback for men.

Sign up for Mimi's mailing list for giveaways and new release news!

STALK MIMI:
www.mimijean.net
pinterest.com/mimijeanromance
instagram.com/mimijeanpamfiloff
facebook.com/MimiJeanPamfiloff